CW01065270

Alphas and Airships

THE RED CAPE SOCIETY, BOOK 2

MELANIE KARSAK

CLOCKPUNK PRESS

❊ Created with Vellum

for Colette

Alphas and Airships

CHAPTER 1
When Werewolves Fly

I clutched the rail of the airship and tried not to look down. My stomach flopped as the vessel rocked in the turbulent air. A raven landed on a nearby rope. It turned and cawed loudly at me.

"Bad omen," the airship balloonman called down from the crow's nest just under the balloon. "Must be getting close."

I waved my hand at the bird, shooing it away.

"Close to what? How can you tell we're close to anything?" I asked, gazing out at the mist-drenched sky. My stomach pitched sideways once more as the airship jostled in the breeze. I inhaled deeply through my nose then exhaled long and slow. Travelling by any means of conveyance save my own feet always brought out the worst in my stomach. But journeying a long distance in an airship? The worst. My mouth watered, and I swallowed hard.

"Close to land. I say, you look green, Agent," the balloonman said.

"I'm fine," I lied then turned and looked back out at the fog.

The balloonman chuckled.

For weeks now, the Scottish division of the Red Cape Society, a unit called Shadow Watch, had reports of a rogue airship trolling the skies above Scotland, the isles, and the North Sea. The pirate ship had been a nuisance at first—as most airship pirates were—but they'd recently attacked Her Majesty's aether armada. They'd lifted a large shipment of weapons and other valuable, but secret, intel from the ship, dropping the sailors in the North Sea as thanks. Our sovereign was not happy.

Airship piracy, even when a nuisance enough to bother Her Majesty, wasn't usually of concern for the Red Cape Society. But one stray report caught the attention of Shadow Watch. One unfortunate bloke, a victim of an attack, washed ashore in Caithness with the story that the pirates had red eyes. Red as rubies.

So here I was, chasing werewolves through the aether.

Captain Martin, who piloted the ship, pulled a cord on his wheelstand. Below deck, a bell rang. Leaning toward a receiver near the wheel, the captain called,

"Slow to coasting." He then looked up at the balloon-man. "Hold her steady."

I dipped into my vest pocket and pulled out a piece of candied ginger. When Grand-mère heard I was headed aloft, she'd insisted I bring the candies along. I was very glad she had. If not for her quick thinking, I'd likely give our location away by retching violently over the side of the airship.

I crossed the deck of the *Jacobite*, a vessel belonging to Her Majesty's aether Navy, and joined Captain Martin.

He unrolled a map. "There was an attack in this area two nights ago. They wait for dense air such as this."

"How do they find the other ships in all this cloud cover?"

"If we descend about fifty feet, we'll fall out of the dense cloud bank. Then, we'd be like ducks in a pond. They must sit in the fog and listen, waiting for their marks to fly past. Typical pirate tactic. They just seem especially good at it—or especially lucky."

Or they have the enhanced hearing of werewolves, I thought, but I didn't say so.

We grew silent as we listened. Below, I heard the sound of the waves. Everything was so still.

Captain Martin was right. If another airship simply sat idle, hidden in a bank of clouds, they could easily hear another craft's gears running. But it also required patience. Thus far, we'd been hunting the pirate craft for the last three hours without any luck.

I glanced at the map the captain was holding. I squinted as I tried to make the image come into focus. I hadn't gotten used to the eyepatch covering my left eye. Fenton's attack had not rendered me completely blind, but it might as well have. My left eye had paled to moon white. All I could see out of that eye were shapes and some stray colors. My right eye was still struggling to keep up with its new burden.

Nor had I quite adjusted to the massive scar across my face. From my brow to my cheek, I now wore a badge of my profession, a gigantic scar from the were-wolf's claws. On top of that, where he had scratched me on my hairline, my black locks had turned white. I stroked my hand across the silvery tuft of fur hanging from my belt. Well, I'd gotten him in the end. Fenton was dead. Under Lionheart's new rule, the realm had been relatively quiet. But there had been a price. I still didn't have a partner. Quinn was barely recovered. I was half blind. And if I'd had bad luck finding a suit-able beau before, now my chances were about zero. My beauty was ruined thanks to Fenton, but at least my hide wasn't hanging from his belt.

I refocused on the map. The elusive pirate ship had been spotted all over the area. However, there had been reports of attacks taking place above the Orcadian and Shetland Islands in the last few days.

"Let's cruise north a little," Captain Martin suggested then rang the galley and signaled to the balloonman.

With a lurch—which made my stomach lurch along with it—the airship moved slowly forward in the fog.

I went to the bow of the ship. Pulling out my new night array optic, I slipped off the simple leather eyepatch I'd been wearing. I winced as my left eye adjusted to the mist-shrouded light. There was a soft glow of gold and pink that made the clouds shimmer as the last rays of sunlight illuminated the skyline. Blinking to adjust my sight, I looked out at the horizon. We were floating inside a cloud.

I looked down at the night optic lens. Master Hart hadn't been able to repair the one Fenton had broken. Keeping in mind the condition of my left eye, he'd made me a new one. It was designed to work in daylight and at night. While it was still handy at night, I felt self-conscious wearing it during the day. Through the blue-tinted day lens, my white eye was still visible.

I was about to slip the lens on when in the far off distance behind us, I heard a pop. And then another.

"Captain?" I called as a flare briefly illuminated the sky.

"Distress flares. I see them, Agent. Hold on," he said

then began to bank the ship sharply. He yanked on the bell to the gear galley. "We need speed. Quickly."

From below the deck of the airship, I heard gears grind as the galleymen prepared to get the airship up to speed.

I grabbed a supporting rope overhead, willed my stomach not to empty itself on the deck of the airship, then squinted in the direction of the flares.

A moment later, I saw a blast of orange light. Through the still air, I heard the sound of voices, yelling, and gunfire.

The *Jacobite* quickly picked up speed. From belowdecks, two Black Watch agents appeared, both of them carrying massive weapons. Lot of good they had been so far. Other than looking nice in their kilts, they'd spent the entire trip playing cards and drinking Scotch. I didn't mind much, just felt a bit jealous be left out.

Sliding the optic back into my pocket, I pulled out my spyglass. Holding on to a rope, I set my right eye on the lens and looked out. It was hard to see through the fog. I saw the silhouette of the ship under attack. There was a shadow in the mist as another ship, the assailant, arrived just off the starboard side of the unlucky vessel. I could see people—just shadows—swinging through the air as they moved off the pirate ship and on to the other vessel.

The *Jacobite* moved quickly toward the scene.

Once more, a raven flew around the *Jacobite*. It circled our vessel then headed back into the mist. As we neared the catastrophe in the making, someone on the pirate ship blew a horn. The long, lonely sound filled the air with its sorrowful call. I scanned the ships. The pirates were shifting goods from the vessel under attack on to their own airship. And the second ship—the one under attack—was beginning to lose altitude.

The horn sounded again.

"Ready the guns," Captain Martin called.

As we neared, I began to feel a tell-tale prickle in the palms of my hands and the bottom of my feet.

I lowered my spyglass and watched.

My mooneye twitched. Out of habit, I closed my right eye—I had always favored the left—and looked. There was definitely something odd about the figures on the deck of the pirate ship. While I couldn't see more than their silhouettes, my bad eye spied an aura of color around them. It quickly became clear that these pirates were not entirely human.

"Now," Captain Martin called.

A moment later, a barrage of bullets rattled from the *Jacobite* toward the pirate vessel.

The horn on the pirate vessel sounded once more. I saw the remaining airship pirates return to their own ship. Then, the pirate ship began to turn away.

Given it was still foggy, and that the sun would drop

from the horizon any minute, soon we'd be chasing pirates in the dark, a prospect that didn't sound a bit appealing.

"They're retreating," I called to Captain Martin.

Captain Martin rang the bell in the gear galley. "We need speed."

"Captain," the balloonman shouted. "The second vessel is a shipping craft. Their balloon just caught on fire. They're going down, sir. All hands still aboard."

"Dammit," the captain swore.

Lifting my spyglass once more, I watched as the pirate airship turned in the opposite direction. As it did so, three things became immediately apparent.

First, like all airships, the balloon had a unique marking. This ship boasted a hammer on the balloon. And on the pommel of that hammer, was a wolf head.

Second, the long, narrow airship boasted a massive figurehead at the prow. As the airship turned away from us, I was able to make out its distinct shape. On the prow of the ship was a wolf.

And finally, if my itching palms and the shadowy colors on the pirates' silhouettes weren't proof enough, when I scanned my spyglass along the vessel, I spotted a hulking figure standing on the rail. While I wasn't able to make out his face, I could see he had long hair which blew in the breeze. His eyes glimmered a dark, wine-red color.

The elusive pirate must have been watching me. He lifted his hand in greeting, then the airship turned, gaining altitude as it went, and disappeared back into the fog.

Meanwhile, the screams from the merchant's vessel quelled out any hope of pursuit. There were innocent people on that ship, and if we didn't move fast to rescue them, they'd soon be swimming.

"Well, there went your pirates, Agent Louvel," the captain called.

"Those weren't pirates," the balloonman corrected.

I looked up at him. "No?"

The man shook his head. "That was a longship. Norse construction. No, sir, not pirates. Those were Vikings."

CHAPTER 2

Agent Edwin Hunter

Frowning at the papers lying in front of me, my head blaring with a headache from trying to see the lines with one bad eye, I tossed my fountain pen onto my desk and leaned back in my seat. I pulled off my eyepatch and pressed the palms of my hands into my eye sockets.

God, I missed Quinn. He always handled the paperwork.

"Agent Louvel," a voice said from behind me. "Enjoying completing your paperwork, I see."

I suppressed a sigh. Agent Hunter, my new boss, seemed particularly keen on ensuring protocol was followed at every turn, including paperwork. I would have completely hated him for it if he had not been so damned good-looking. Quickly grabbing my eyepatch, I pulled it back on then rose.

"Of course, Agent Hunter. What else is there to live for in life?" I said, turning to look at him. I wasn't sure I had ever seen so fine a specimen of a man in my entire life. His yellow hair was perfectly coifed, his mutton-chops neat and tidy, his suit well-tailored to accentuate every perfect curve of his body. If he had not been so tightly wound, and my boss, and so much out of my league, he would be perfect. My eyes drifted to his. They were sky blue. No. He was perfect. I was the one who was a mess.

"Other than chasing flying werewolves? I hate to take you from your report—I see you're quite engrossed —but would you mind joining me in my office?"

In your office. On your desk. What? Good lord, Clemeny. He's your boss. "I, um, sure."

"Very well," he said with a nod. He placed his hands behind his back, and together, we headed toward his office.

I eyed the other agents as we went. Headquarters was unusually busy. There must have been at least four dozen agents in-house that morning, most of them at their desks working. Many of them looked up, giving Agent Hunter semi-annoyed glances.

Ah. They were here filling out reports too. No wonder it was so busy and so grumpy.

Agent Greystock had always let us slip a little, giving a little latitude where necessary—and sometimes even when it wasn't. Agent Hunter, however, didn't just go by the book, he might have actually written it.

"I reviewed your preliminary field notes. Plans for follow-up?" Agent Hunter asked.

"Yes, sir. I noted the marking on the balloon, and the airship had a distinct masthead. I'll begin checking port records then asking some questions at the London and Edinburgh Towers. I need to see who knows what about this airship crew and is willing to talk."

Agent Hunter nodded. "And you are certain that these were preternatural pirates?"

I nodded. "Yes. As we expected, they were wolves, sir."

"How do you know? Were they shifted?"

"No. It's all in the eyes. Werewolves always have a spark of red in the eyes. They can't hide it. And, well, I was just sure. They aren't doing much to hide it," I said then pulled out my tablet, flipping to the sketch I had made of the sigil on the balloon of the airship. I handed it to Agent Hunter.

"The balloon emblem?"

I nodded. "And on the masthead of the ship was a wolf."

Agent Hunter stroked his chin. "The Hammer of Thor."

"The Hammer of Thor?"

He nodded. "The symbol is not just any hammer.

This shape… It's Norse. This is the Hammer of Thor married with the image of the wolf's head."

I smirked then shook my head. "Vikings."

Agent Hunter looked at me.

"Just something one of the crew of the *Jacobite* said. He called them Vikings, not pirates. Their airship had an unusual, longship design. That, coupled with the wolf symbols—Vikings."

Agent Hunter nodded. "Seems he was right."

We arrived at Agent Hunter's office. A craftsman was working on the door, removing Agent Greystock's name.

"I have no doubt you'll get a handle on your Vikings. I have reviewed your file, Agent Louvel, and you are a highly accomplished field agent. You and Agent Briarwood were quite the pair to be reckoned with. I understand Her Majesty awarded you a special commendation for your work in the recent Marlowe case."

"Yes, sir." Indeed, she had. I wasn't much impressed with the bonus at the time—given I was nearly blind in one eye, a colleague was dead, and my partner had just quit—but I was able to buy Grand-mère a new bed with the extra coin, so in the end, I had appreciated the gesture. Her Majesty had even sent along a bauble, a silver and onyx broach, to honor my service. Quinn had been given one too. I didn't know whether or not Agent

Rose had also received any kind of recognition for her—and Constantine's—part in the case. I hadn't seen her since.

"Given how accomplished you are in the field, it seems foolish to have you wasting your time chasing down small details, interviewing people. I have assigned you a new partner, on a temporary basis, for this case."

My stomach dropped to my feet. *Oh. God. No.*

"Your new partner can work on any minutia at your discretion. I have also sent word to my counterparts at Shadow Watch. That division's aid is entirely at your disposal, including the *Jacobite*."

"Thank you. And my new partner?" My mind quickly went down the list of people Agent Hunter might have paired with me. I grew increasingly despairing as I thought it over. This was not the right time to train a rookie.

Agent Hunter smiled, motioned to the workman who stepped aside, then we entered his office.

There, I found junior Agent Harper.

"I believe the two of you already know one another," Agent Hunter said.

I breathed an audible sigh of relief. Okay, at least it was just Harper. But still. "Agent Harper, I'm surprised. I thought you wanted to work in—"

"In administration. I know. I'm going to try some

field rotations. I thought… It's just… I always admired you and Quinn. When the opportunity arose to work with you, I applied. I won't get in your way, Clemeny. I promise."

I chuckled. "It's not me you need to worry about. Get your things, Agent Harper. We're headed out now."

"Out? Out were?"

"First stop, of course, is the big, bad wolf," I said, turning to pass Agent Hunter a playful wink only to realize a stupid truth. I wink with my left eye. Instead, I made a strange, half-squinting but slightly flirtatious— yet ugly—face at him.

Agent Hunter raised an eyebrow at me but then chuckled softly, an honest and endearing smile crossing his face for just a moment.

It was the sweetest thing I'd seen with my one good eye all week.

CHAPTER 3
Ragnarok

The sound of the squash ball hitting the wall was audible even before we slipped into the viewing box at the back of the court. The sport, which had never much appealed to me, was all the rage these days. When we opened the door to enter the viewing room, Agent Harper and I were surprised to find a pair of King's College students inside. Deeply engrossed in one another, they didn't even notice us.

I cleared my throat.

"Room's taken, bugger off—" the *gentleman* began but then turned and looked at Agent Harper and me.

The moment he caught sight of our red capes, his expression changed.

He whispered to the girl then took her hand. The pair slipped past us, giving us sidelong glances and a wide berth.

"I've worn the cape for eighteen months. Still haven't gotten used to being treated like a leper," Agent Harper grumbled.

I smirked. "It's better this way. Now we have the place to ourselves."

"Fabulous spot for a cuddle though."

"Isn't it?" I replied with a smirk, slipping inside. The viewer's box was narrow and had a low ceiling. All in all, it felt a bit like a confessional. The place was congested, smelling heavily of dust and the wafting tang of sweat from the squash court. And just below that, I caught Lionheart's musky scent.

I inhaled slowly, feeling the strange flush that came over me whenever Lionheart was around. I sighed. *Seriously, I needed to find a man.*

Much to my surprise, Agent Hunter and his honest smile passed through my mind.

A grin played on my lips.

"What is it?" Agent Harper asked.

I shook my head. "Nothing."

"Is that him?" Agent Harper asked, motioning to Lionheart.

I nodded.

"I saw him just once before, but at a distance. He was talking to Her Majesty."

I nodded then watched as Lionheart and Bryony Paxton moved quickly, volleying the squash ball back and forth, and trying to outsmart one another in the process. Bryony's blond hair, which she'd pulled into a bun, was coming loose. Strands of golden hair trailed down from her temples. Her face was flushed red from the exertion, but she was smiling all the same. All in all, she looked very pretty. Happy, even. Very happy.

I sighed softly, my eyes going to Lionheart. I watched his moves. To my surprise, he wasn't holding back—much. He probably could have hit the squash ball hard enough to make it explode, but as I watched his arm muscles flex, I realized he was using more strength just to control his lupine energy, keeping the match fair. But at the same time, Bryony was no slouch. Her hits were solid, slick, and sometimes, a little dirty.

They were actually well-matched.

Lucky girl. No wonder she looked so happy.

"He's not so bad to look at," Agent Harper whispered to me. "Especially in his fitness pants."

Lionheart cast a quick glance over his shoulder.

"One thing you need to understand about werewolves is that they have exceptionally good ears."

Agent Harper's cheeks flushed pink, her embarrassment showing up quickly on her fair, peaches and cream complexion. It must be troublesome to be a redhead. They never seemed able to hide their blush on those pale cheeks.

"Don't worry. I don't think Sir Richard minds a lady

noticing how firm he is," I said with a grin, fully aware that Lionheart could hear. "Have you noticed his calves, for example? Have you ever seen such perfect speci- mens?" And, as I had hoped, my comment had thrown him off, distracting him from the match.

"Point," Bryony cheered. "And, that's match," she added, her hands on her hips as she grinned at her part- ner. Her breath was ragged, but she was beaming at Lionheart.

"Are they?" Agent Harper whispered in an almost inaudible voice to me.

I looked at her then raised a playful eyebrow.

"Well, Agent Louvel, you've cost me the match. Why don't you come out and join us?" Lionheart said, turning to the box.

Bryony's brow flexed in confusion as she turned around.

I motioned to Agent Harper, and we exited the low door that led out into the squash court.

"Clemeny," Bryony said, moving to greet me. "I'd embrace you, but I smell like an old sock," she said with a laugh, pausing to kiss me on both cheeks. "Good to see you."

"And you," I said, then looked to Lionheart. "Sir Richard."

"Agent Louvel," he said with a smirk then cast a glance back at Agent Harper. "Agent Harper, correct?"

"I-um-yes. Pleased to meet you, sir."

"How is Agent Briarwood?" Lionheart asked, turning away from Agent Harper.

Out of the corner of my eye, I saw Agent Harper frown at being ignored so easily. It would take time for Lionheart to get used to her.

"On his feet, which is about as much as we can ask for, for now."

"Very good."

"I have a couple of questions if you have time," I said.

"And I'm sure you have the same questions even if I don't."

I grinned.

"I'll go wash up. Meet you in the commons?" Bryony said to Lionheart. I cast her a glance, realizing that her cheerful smile had deflated somewhat.

"Sorry. Just business. It won't take long," I told her. While my heart thumped in my chest every time Lionheart beamed his smile—especially his smirky half-smile—at me, if Bryony Paxton had a claim to the were-wolf's heart, I would never do anything to disrespect that. I might really want someone of my own, but only a bitch—literally and figuratively—gets in between a woman and her man—er, werewolf.

Bryony nodded. She reached out for Lionheart's

hand and gave it a little squeeze then headed toward a side door.

Motioning for me to come along with him, Lionheart picked up Bryony's racquet and headed toward the rack on the other side of the room.

I motioned to Agent Harper to stay behind.

"Quite unfair of you, *Little Red*," Lionheart said as we crossed the court. "Now I have to pick up the tab for dinner."

"Whatever are you talking about?" I asked with a grin.

Lionheart huffed a laugh. "Agent Harper then?"

"Trial period."

Lionheart harrumphed again.

"Don't think she'll work out?"

"Perhaps you should guide her toward something else."

"Are you offering me advice?"

"Perhaps."

"Hmm," I mused. "Speaking of advice, perhaps you should tone down that wolfy smirk. Might accidentally make the woman who loves you feel jealous."

"The woman who loves me?" Lionheart said, stopping cold.

Didn't he realize? "Just a suggestion."

"Duly noted. So, what can I do for you today, Agent Louvel? As far as I know, everything is quiet."

"So it is, on the ground," I said then pulled out my sketch of the airship. "It's the aether I'm worried about."

"Aether? Does Her Majesty have you chasing Valkyries?"

"Not quite," I said, handing the sketch to Lionheart.

He slipped the racquets back into the rack then took the drawing pad from me. He studied the image. "Where did you see this symbol?"

"On the balloon of an airship prowling the North Sea."

Lionheart grunted that low, quiet, and very were-wolf-like noise that always surprised me. "These are mixed symbols. This is the Hammer of Thor," he said, his finger tracing the sketch. "But this is the symbol of Fenrir," he said, pointing to the wolf's head on the pommel of the hammer.

"Fenrir?"

"Fenrir the wolf. Don't you know your Norse mythology, Agent Louvel?"

"No, but I did save a bear named Loki once."

Lionheart smirked. "Fenrir the wolf was the son of Loki. The Asgardian gods raised Fenrir. But when he grew too large, too dangerous, they chained him. During Ragnarok, Fenrir the wolf escaped. The wolf swallowed the sun and killed Odin himself."

"That's cheerful."

"Clemeny, the Norse werewolf packs are not to be trifled with. The worship of the wolf is steeped deep within their culture and religion. Werewolves, such as Fenrir, were worshipped as gods. There was a time when there were nearly as many werewolves as there were men in their lands. That was part of the reason the Vikings were so strong, so successful," Lionheart said then sneered.

"Viking werewolves. Fabulous."

Lionheart handed my notepad back to me. "I'll make inquiries."

"I'm headed back to Scotland. Shadow Watch was kind enough to offer to ferry me through the clouds."

"While I admire your abundant bravery, *Little Red*, don't forget you can't fly."

"How do you know? Maybe I smell like roses because I'm secretly a Valkyrie. I might sprout some celestial wings and prevent the next Ragnarok."

"Didn't you just tell me not to flirt?"

"Who's flirting?"

Lionheart laughed. "Be careful up there, Agent Louvel."

"Thank you, Sir Richard."

With a nod, I turned and rejoined Agent Harper. The pair of us headed back outside.

"Well, seems Sir Richard hasn't warmed up to me yet," Agent Harper said.

"He will. Give him time."

"I didn't mind. The view from where I was standing was divine."

I laughed. "Careful. Don't forget, he bites."

"I certainly hope so."

CHAPTER 4

The Dís

P er Agent Hunter's advice, I sent Harper to the London airship towers while I headed in a different direction. Over the years, Quinn had managed to make a good network of informants. Most of them had come to trust me as well. Except Alodie. The bitch. When Lionheart took control, I'd suggested to him that Alodie be shipped off to Australia as well, but Lionheart disagreed—albeit reluctantly. The two of them had never gotten along. Her tarty ways might have been fine for Cyril, but they did not mesh with the morals of the Templars. Lionheart let her stay in London on the condition she close the brothel and stay out of the way. She'd agreed and had been quiet ever since. Her silence, however, did not convince me that she was to be trusted. After all, she had sold out Quinn. She denied it. But one expects that from a bitch.

Alodie would be no help here, but I knew someone who might. If she would talk.

Making a quick stop first, I headed across town to Canterbury Row. The street, which had once been fashionable, had fallen into disrepair. Sitting on the very edge of one of London's dark districts, a place where the preternatural frequently roamed, the aura around the street seemed to keep the human patrons away. Still, small shops lined the place, most of which looked as if they hadn't seen a customer in ages.

I paused outside the small bookshop and looked up at the sign: *The Norns' Eddas*. The letters had been written in a font that looked more rune than alphabet.

I headed inside.

The bell above the door rang as I entered.

I was immediately overcome by the scent of old books, dust, and incense.

I cast a glance around. Everywhere I looked, I saw books, scrolls, and other odds and ends. Nearly unidentifiable skeletons sat under glass. I threw a wary eye at a handmade mobile that hung above the door. It was made of bones, black feathers, and mirrors. On the floor was a circle with runes drawn within it.

"I knew you were coming," a scratchy female voice called from the back of the room

"Well, that's easy to say." I eyed the eerie circle then stepped out of it. It wasn't intended for me. I headed toward the back of the shop. Tracing my fingers along the bookcase, I made a line of dust. I flicked the dust from my fingers. "Maid take the year off?"

There was a cackling laugh. "I like your jokes, Clemeny Louvel."

"I'm delighted to hear that," I said as I reached the back. There, a small flight of steps led to a raised platform. Bookcases lined the walls, but at a small table in one corner sat an ancient woman in an old velvet gown that was fraying visibly at the seams. She had long, curly silver hair that was a tangled mess. On the small table before her was an oil lamp, a yellow scroll, and a heap of bones. She gave me a toothy grin as she looked up at me with her rheumy eyes.

"By Freya, he did a number on you, didn't he? You're almost as blind as me," she said with a laugh.

I huffed a laugh then climbed the steps to join her.

"Doesn't have much to say about it now though, do you, Fenton?" I asked, patting the pelt.

At that, she laughed. "No, he doesn't. Quite silent. Quite silent. You want me to call him up? We can ask him what he thinks," she said, reaching for the pile of bones.

I shook my head. "No, thanks."

"No, of course not. You're not here for him. You're here to find out about the son of Skoll."

I took a seat. Thank the gods—hers, mine,

whomever—that she was in the mood to talk today. There were times when Quinn and I visited the Dís only to find her sitting unmoving, unspeaking, for months. But luckily, not today.

"I'll bite. Who's Skoll."

"Skoll chases Mani."

"Okay, that's not helpful."

The Dís laughed. "Agent Louvel, you always say the funniest things."

"I'm glad you think so."

"Skoll and Hati were wolves, brothers, sons of Fenrir. Hati chased Sol, the sun, and became a man. Skoll chased Mani, the moon, and your enemies were born. I have seen you in the clouds, chasing the son of Skoll."

Now we were getting somewhere. "Who is he? Where can I find him?"

The Dís pressed her lips together and hummed. She picked up the bones with her ancient hands and held them out to me.

"Bleed now so you will not bleed later," she told me.

Sighing, I pulled my knife from my belt. Cutting my finger, I dripped blood onto the bones. For the briefest of moments, I could have sworn I saw a flash of gold.

The Dís laughed then tossed the bones on the table before her. She then dug into the pocket of her old gown and pulled out a feather. Moving slowly, she held it above her lamp until it smoked. She wafted the smoke over the bones, bathing them in the pungent air. She then began to intone lightly. As she spoke, her eyes rolled, revealing only the whites of her eyes.

Curious, I pulled off my eyepatch and looked at the bones.

"Yes, you look, Clemeny Louvel. You look with your new eye," the Dís said then chanted some more.

I stared at the bones until my vision blurred and faded. An image appeared before me. It was murky at first, almost cloudy in the mist. I heard a raven caw, and slowly, an image came into view. It wasn't just the vision I saw that made things cloudy. It was actually clouds. My eyes settled on a man who was standing at the prow of an airship. The massive wolf's head on the masthead pushed through the clouds. The man stared into the distance, his eyes glimmering red. He had long, blond hair and his arms were covered with tattoos, including the Hammer of Thor married with the wolf's head.

"Captain Skollson," someone called from behind him.

The man didn't look around.

"Zayde?"

The man frowned, looking annoyed. "What?"

"Sorry, sir. We found something interesting amongst

the log of the *Perceval*. We thought you should have a look."

The captain looked out at the sky. The airship moved out of the clouds, pushing into the clear blue sky. A cool wind whipped off the dark waves below. The captain closed his eyes, seeming to relish the breeze on his face.

"For Fenrir," he whispered, then turned back to his ship.

The Dís snapped her fingers, and the image faded.

I looked up at her.

"Son of Skoll," she said. "You see."

"I do. But why is he here?"

"When one king's reign ends, and a new reign begins, they will all test the mettle of the new ruler. The son of Skoll smells blood in the wind."

"The changing of alpha," I said.

She nodded. "He may be the first, but he will not be the last. Until the Lion shows his teeth, they will all come."

"Wonderful. So I'm doing Lionheart's dirty work."

The Dís laughed. "And he hasn't done yours?"

"True." I rose.

"Did you forget my fee, Clemeny Louvel?" the Dís asked.

I smiled. "Of course not."

Reaching into my pocket, I pulled out a small box and set it on the table before her.

"Belgian or French?"

"French, of course."

She lifted the lid, revealing the chocolates inside. The fine quality confections had set me back a day's wages, but you get what you pay for. And the Dís's fee was always worth the price.

"Felice Louvel has taught you well," she said as her fingers waggled over the chocolates. "Excellent taste."

I smothered a frown. After Fenton, I didn't want any of them to know anything about my grand-mère. But at least the Dís wasn't dangerous.

"Thank you," I told her, pushing in my chair.

She inclined her head to me then took a chocolate from the box. "Raspberry," she said, looking it over.

"What, you can see inside the chocolates as well? Prophetic about the taste?" I asked with a grin.

She laughed. "No, you stupid girl, there is a key printed on the inside of the lid."

I looked at the box. So there was. I laughed. "Enjoy."

"I shall. Be careful when you are north of old Hadrian's wall, Clemeny Louvel. The son of Skoll travels with his fylgja. But when you need them, remember that the old ones will always shelter those with the right blood. Those like you."

I turned and looked back at her. "And just what is a fylgja?"

She chuckled. "You'll figure it out."

"Prophets. Always riddling," I said with a grin.

"I'm no prophet. I am Dís," she said with a laugh, her mouth full of chocolate.

Chuckling, I turned and headed outside.

Well, Zayde Skollson—and your fylgja, whatever that was—it was time for you to learn that this realm has teeth.

CHAPTER 5

The Graveyard Shift

The agency airship lifted off from the roof of headquarters, ferrying Agent Harper and me to Edinburgh.

"Three sightings," Agent Harper said as she settled onto the bench beside me.

Chewing my candied ginger, which I really should have bought more of when I stopped at the confectionary, I willed my stomach not to pay attention to the way the airship gondola rocked in the breeze.

"There have probably been more, but, of course, no one wanted to talk to me. I bribed a few people. Is that okay?" Agent Harper asked. While it was an honest question, her green eyes smiled mischievously. Maybe she was more suited to field work than she thought.

I nodded. "File them on form 71-B for a reimbursement."

"71-B? On the expenses sheet? Seriously?"

I nodded.

Agent Harper chuckled then turned back to her notes. "I suppose as long as I file my paperwork, Agent Hunter will be satisfied. All right, so there is a merchant vessel that ships Scotch between a distillery in the highlands and London. Your pirate airship has tried to catch them on two occasions. The airship is heavily armed but only got away by chance on both occasions. Once, due to a freak lightning storm, and the second time because the pirate ship retreated."

"Retreated? That's odd. All right, what else?"

"Now, the second story was from a pilot who runs transports. He's a courier, quick trip chap, pilots an old racing airship. Of course, I don't know if his tale is fact or fable, but he talked about the pirate airship like it was a ghost vessel. I don't know. Maybe he just made up the story. It sounded too unbelievable."

"Well, we are talking about an airship full of werewolves. Could anything sound less believable?"

Agent Harper laughed. "You're right. It was the bit about the ravens, I guess."

"The ravens?"

She nodded. "The pirate said he was pretty high aloft when a flock of ravens suddenly surrounded his ship."

"An unkindness."

"Sorry?"

"A flock of ravens is called an unkindness or a conspiracy."

"How do you know that?"

"Quinn," I said with a smile, suddenly missing my old partner.

"All right. Well, an unkindness of ravens appeared. He also spotted the wolf masthead. I think it spooked them."

"How did he get away?"

"Cut altitude and raced through a pass of rocks at sea level. He said he pushed the old racing ship to its limit, damaged the rudder in the process. They were at the repair tower."

"Why would the pirate ship attack a courier? What was he carrying?"

"Yeah, he clammed up when I asked. He muttered something about the Earl of Derby, but wouldn't divulge more."

"I see. And the last ship?"

"Scottish craft. The crew was Shetlandic. From what I understood, they spotted the pirate airship near Fair Isle. They gave the ship a wide berth and escaped unscathed."

"Fair Isle."

"A tiny little isle in the Shetlands. Mostly unin-habited."

"Sounds like a good place to hide out."

"Exactly what I was thinking."

"Well done, Agent Harper."

She beamed a little. "Thank you, Clemeny. I was supposed to go on rotation next month with Cressida, but when I overheard some talk about assigning you a new partner, I jumped. I just… I hope I can do a good job."

"So far, so good. No one's dead yet, and we have a lead. Let's see what they know at Shadow Watch, and we'll go from there."

"What about you? Any luck?"

"Some. I know the name of the man we're hunting."

Harper's mouth dropped open a little before she caught herself. "What? How?"

"Well, we'll get into the details of that later."

"Okay, then who are we after?"

"His name is Zayde Skollson."

Harper turned a page in her notebook and jotted the name down. "Norwegian," she said as she tapped her pen on her journal. "Skollson… Son of Skoll. Wasn't Skoll one of the Norse gods?"

"Apparently Skoll was a wolf."

"Well, that makes sense."

"You know your Norse gods?"

"A bit."

"What's a fylgja?"

"Fylgja? I have no idea. Why? Do you know what it is?"

I shook my head. "No, that's why I was asking you. Whatever it is, it's probably going to try to kill us, so if we can figure it out first, that will be helpful."

Harper laughed. "Noted. I also sent along a runner. I've secured us rooms in Holyrood House Inn so we can get some rest tonight."

"Ah," I mused then grinned at her. "Agent Harper, I have some very bad news for you."

"And that is?"

"Werewolf hunters rarely sleep. And we never sleep at night."

"Oh," Agent Harper said then looked off into the distance.

For the first time, I saw her enthusiasm for the job dim.

I chuckled. "But I suppose I can let you rest for a few hours. From here on out, it's the graveyard shift."

"All right."

"Now, we may not sleep, but we do drink. After that terrible news, the first round tonight is on me," I said, giving her a gentle slap on the back.

My stomach, however, reminded me that I needed to get back on the ground first before I started thinking of putting anything in my stomach. I pulled the brown paper packet of sugared ginger from my pocket and popped another confection.

Well, one thing was sure, I was most definitely motivated to get this case over and done with. I had never been so nauseated in all my life.

CHAPTER 6
Meat and Potatoes

Much to my relief, the airship arrived in port just as my sugared ginger had taken me as far as they could go. I consented to let Agent Harper check us in at Holyrood House Inn where my stomach could get a few minutes rest before the night began.

Holyrood House Inn was an old Tudor-style building along the Royal Mile not far from the airship towers. All in all, the place was quiet enough and clean. The maid led us upstairs to two adjoining rooms. I took the one that overlooked the street. It was always good to have options for a getaway.

"I spotted a pub down the way. Horse something. Meet you there in two hours?" I asked Agent Harper as she headed into her own room.

"All right. We're expected at Shadow Watch whenever we're ready."

I nodded but didn't say anything more. The agency always wanted us to report in here or file a report there. Shadow Watch, the Scottish Division, probably wanted to know what, exactly, we were up to. Agent Greystock had always been good about letting Quinn and me roam wherever we needed. We got the job done. That was all that mattered, in the end. Agent Hunter had been on the job for a couple of months now. He was a stickler for formality and procedure, but aside from making me fill out lengthy reports—which were really part of the job anyway—he hadn't gotten in my way.

I entered my room. Aside from the tidily made bed, the narrow room had a dressing table, chair, wardrobe, and washstand. At once, I extinguished the lamp. It was almost dark. It wouldn't do to have anyone glancing this way. I checked the wardrobe—never hurt to be safe —then looked out the window.

Edinburgh, like London, was a busy hub. Everywhere I looked, I saw horses, carriages, autos, velocipedes, and steambikes. But what was on the ground hardly mattered. It was what was up in the sky that was the real problem.

My stomach reminded me then that going back into the clouds was the last thing it wanted.

I flopped down on the bed. Pulling out my small pocket watch, I looked at the time. It was nearly seven. I closed my eyes. Once more, Agent Hunter came to mind. I remembered his slight, honest smile. Reaching up, I pulled off the eyepatch covering my mooneye. My fingertips lightly touched the scar on my face. I had been pretty. But now? I sighed. I closed my eyes and pushed the dark thoughts away. It didn't matter how sweetly Agent Hunter had smiled. I was an inferior at work and a werewolf hunter with a mangled face. At this rate, I was going to have a hard time attracting even the likes of Pastor Frank.

Shut it, Clemeny. There's got to be someone out there for you.

Even Lionheart had someone. I swallowed the jealousy that wanted to wash up in me when I thought of Bryony Paxton. Hell, if I couldn't even win a preternatural, was there any hope? I closed my eyes and willed myself not to think on it anymore. I needed to sleep. It was going to be a long night.

I DOZED OFF LONG ENOUGH FOR MY STOMACH TO RECOVER. I woke feeling hungry and thirsty. My meal that day had consisted primarily of ginger. I needed real food.

Lots of it. Dreaming of Scotch pie and a pint, I washed my face and headed out. Lingering by Agent Harper's door, I heard her snoring loudly inside.

I chuckled. Agent Harper, who was a very pretty girl —petite, red-haired, green-eyed—snored like a lumberjack. From the sounds of it, she could use a bit more rest. Planning to return in a couple of hours, I left her at the inn then made my way down the busy street to The White Horse Pub.

When I entered, a few people gave me and my red cape a sidelong glance, but no one said anything. I found a seat at the end of the bar where I could keep an eye on the door.

"What will you have, lass?" the bartender asked, his voice thick with a Scottish accent.

I turned to find myself face-to-face with a brown-haired, brown eyed, beauty. From his square jaw to his massive biceps, he was a sight to behold.

"Your best stout and a Scotch pie."

The bartender inclined his head to me. "Of course," he said then whistled at another attendant, made a hand gesture, and turned to the tap.

"What was that?" I asked.

"What was what?" he replied as he began pouring.

"This," I said, replicating the move he'd made with his hands.

He chuckled then set my pint down in front of me. The black liquid had a soft, caramel-colored head. Perfect. "Well, you almost had it right. But the way you did it, you ordered extra potatoes on the side."

"Extra potatoes?"

The bartender nodded. "Johannes is deaf. We have a system for handling the kitchen orders."

"Oh. Well, maybe I wanted extra potatoes."

He chuckled. "I'm Ronald," he said, inclining his head to me.

"Clemeny."

"I don't remember seeing you here before, Clemeny."

"That line sounds tired. Want to try a different one?"

Ronald laughed. "All right. Don't see many Red Capes in here. Up from London?"

"That's better. Yes, I am."

"And what is it, exactly, you people do? Aren't you some sort of constable?"

"Something like that."

"Tough job?"

"At times," I said, tapping my cheek below my eye patch.

"Just another day on the job? What happened, tangle with a bear?"

"Wolf, actually."

"Sure," he said then gave me a wink. "One moment," he said then turned and went to the small window that looked back toward the kitchen. He waved to someone then made another motion with his hands. After, he returned once more.

I cocked an eyebrow at him.

He grinned. "Anyone who takes on a wolf for the greater good of the realm is certainly deserving of a side of potatoes. On the house," he said with a grin, and then went to wait on another patron.

My stomach, which had been doing nauseated flips all days, turned once more. But this time, with a strange, excited hope. Not two hours ago I had given up hope of love forever. A brawny Scottish tapster would work just fine, thank you.

As I sipped my pint, I suddenly became aware of a strange tingling in the palms of my hands. Scanning the room, I spotted a tall man at the very back of the pub. He was talking to a pretty girl who appeared to be part of an airship crew. I eyed him carefully, letting all my senses come to me.

Not a wolf.

But not a human either.

The man smiled at the girl, but he quickly passed me a look.

He had strange eyes. Even from this distance, I saw how they sparkled. They were not the mirrored silver of a vampire's eyes. Nor were they the red of a werewolf. Too tall to be a goblin. Too well-built to be a ghoul.

The man excused himself from his pretty female companion for a moment and went to the bar at the other end of the pub. He spoke to Ronald, and a moment later, the tapster handed him two glasses of Scotch. To my surprise, the man crossed the room and came to stand in front of me. He set the drink down on the bar before me.

"Er ye lookin' fer me?" He had a deep, thick accent and something about the way he rolled his words told me that whomever he was, he'd been around for a very long time. He eyed me warily. It suddenly occurred to me that he was deciding whether or not to murder me right then and there.

"Not unless you're a werewolf."

He chuckled. "Then we should be at peace. I dinna come fer trouble, Agent. Just fer a drink."

"Same," I said then lifted the Scotch. "I'm hunting flying werewolves. Any chance you've seen any?"

"Hmm," the man said rubbing his chin. "Air is nary my element. But if I see any swimmin', I'll let ye know."

I smirked. He was a kelpie. That explained the eyes. "Bit landlocked, aren't you?"

"Not t'all," he said then lifted his drink. "I'll be swimmin' soon enough."

I laughed then inclined my head to him.

He nodded then clicked his glass against mine. We both drank. But as I did so, I felt someone else's gaze on me. The girl the kelpie had been talking to was glaring daggers at me.

"I think you better swim back across the pub. Your sweetheart is getting the wrong idea. I assume you have no intentions of pulling her under."

"Ne'er. Only und'r the sheets," he said with a laugh.

I laughed. "Very well. Carry on. And who am I thanking for this drink?"

He inclined his head to me. "Eideard."

"Thank you, Eideard. It's was a mighty fine Scotch. I'm Agent Louvel."

"Well met," he said then inclined his head to me.

Looking around him, I waved at the girl who glared at me.

Eideard gave me a smile then headed back across the pub to the girl who had gone into a full pout. Her arms crossed, her gaze moody and distant, I marveled at her ability to so deftly shame a man while also looking stunningly beautiful. Maybe the reason I still didn't have a beau was because I was decidedly unskilled in the art of the hunt. Werewolves? No problem. An eligible bachelor? Not so much.

Speaking of.

"Here you are," Ronald said when he returned with my plate. The Scotch pie was sided by a massive heap of potatoes, and the entire meal was slathered in rich beef gravy.

"Heaven on a plate."

"You haven't even tasted it yet. How do you know?"

"I can just tell," I said with a grin.

Ronald chuckled. "Nice to see a lady with an appetite," he said with a smile, and then turned to wait on another patron.

My utensil heaped with a massive bite of potatoes and gravy, I paused. Wasn't it Lord Byron who said that watching a lady eat was vulgar? Or was it Percy Shelley who'd said that? Twats both. I remembered thinking that comment the stupidest thing I'd ever heard. I looked at the potatoes. Okay, maybe I wasn't as refined as Grand-mère might hope, but I was hungry. And I was on the job.

I stuck the bite into my mouth. Salty, beefy, and starchy. Divine.

I sighed then got lost in my plate.

I WAS ON MY THIRD STOUT, WHICH GIVEN I'D ALSO HAD A Scotch, was one too many, when I realized that my level of flirtation with Ronald the tapster was getting quite ridiculous. I also realized that Agent Harper had never shown up. It was one thing to get distracted on the job because something was trying to kill you. It was quite another to get distracted by drink and bulging biceps.

I had just risen and was setting some coins down on the bar when Roland returned.

"Leaving?" he asked. I thought I heard some disappointment in his voice, but I wasn't quite sure. My instincts invariably failed me in this department.

"Need to meet my partner," I said, motioning toward the door. Assuming I hadn't already left her to an untimely death while I was busy dreaming of snogging a handsome tapster.

He nodded then pushed my coins back toward me. "On the house. As thanks for whatever it is you do on behalf of the realm."

I cast a glance back toward where the kelpie and his girl had been hovering. They'd already cleared out. Off for some swimming, I supposed.

I could do with a bit of swimming myself.

Smiling at Roland, I said, "Thank you."

He inclined his head toward me. "It was nice to meet you, Clemeny."

"You too."

"I... I'm here most nights."

Don't say something stupid. Don't say something stupid. "Then I'll be back for more potatoes."

And you said something stupid. Well done.

He smirked. "Good."

With a little wave before I said anything else wholly ridiculous, I headed outside.

Now, I had two problems to consider. First, I had very likely left Agent Harper behind to her certain doom. And two, I was the worst flirt ever. Seriously. Potatoes?

CHAPTER 7

The Dark District

O ne should never, ever drink too much on the job. That was one of the first things Quinn told me. In general, I was more for tea than ale, but between the Scotch, the stout, and the allure of the tapster, I found my head was far too swimmy for my own good. I cursed myself as I headed back to the inn. My balance was still a bit off due to the eyepatch. I realized I was zigzagging down the street like the local drunk. Wonderful. I pulled off my eye patch and steadied myself.

The risk of being killed by a werewolf was not worth the flirtation. And besides, even when lusty images of Ronald the tapster came to mind, I found myself thinking about how getting involved in such nonsense would reflect on me. I didn't want Agent Hunter to have any reason to think poorly of me.

Cursing myself for my stupidity, I headed back toward the inn.

The Edinburgh airship towers were alive with light. Ships flew in and out of the busy port. I stopped and eyed the markings on all of the balloons. No sign of Thor's Hammer.

"You won't find her there," a voice called from the alley on the opposite side of the street.

At once, my stomach twisted with knots, and the palms of my hands prickled.

Hell's bells, I had drunk so much my sixth sense was off.

I turned and looked toward the alley. To my surprise, with my mooneye, I saw a reddish glow surrounding the person—well, werewolf—leaning against the building.

I stared at the man.

Just as I had seen in my vision, he had long blond hair braided at the temples and an equally long beard. His tattooed arms were crossed on his chest. He wore striped pants and a heavy tunic.

"Why are you looking for me, Agent Louvel?" he asked. His voice was deep and dusky, thick with a Norwegian accent.

"Am I looking for you?"

"You're looking for the *Fenrir*. I've seen you up there," he said, tilting his chin toward the sky.

"Perhaps I am, Zayde Skollson."

He paused. I could see from his expression that he was surprised that I knew his name. "*Perhaps* you'd better find something else to do. Keep your nose on the ground with the professor and out of the aether. We have our own business aloft, and it had nothing to do with you."

"By business, I suppose you mean piracy," I said, taking a step closer to him so I could see him better. I saw the glint of gold hanging from one ear.

He smirked. *Why do they always smirk?* "Just a hustle or two. Nothing to be concerned about."

"Ah, but that's where you're wrong. Her Majesty was rather put out about her ship. And I really don't like hearing of citizens ending up in the drink for a hustle."

The werewolf stepped toward me. He really was a massive creature. "And what are you going to do to stop me?"

"Why, anything I can, of course."

"Lionheart doesn't rule the skies. There's a different alpha in the aether. Fenrir is lord there, and I am his son. Stay away, or you'll pay the price."

I ran my hand across the pelt hanging on my belt. "Funny. Fenton told me something quite similar. Didn't you, old boy," I said, patting the fur. "And we all know how that turned out."

The werewolf's gaze grew steely. "I won't let you get in my way."

"Then I guess we have a problem."

The werewolf straightened then looked gravely at me. "It's not worth dying over, Agent Louvel," he said then quickly shifted form into a wolf. His fur was a light gold color. He looked at me, his eyes blazing red. A moment later, he turned and loped down the alley.

And like a fool, I went after him.

First, this was very likely a trick. Chances were good I was being led somewhere, presumably so I could be either killed or abducted. If not, I wanted to at least see where the werewolf had headed. If he wasn't docking his airship at the Edinburgh towers, then where had he stashed his ship? Once again running in the direction of the monster—stupid, really—I headed into the alley. As I raced ahead, I pulled out my new night optic array. I slid it on and activated the device. A green light glowed, and a moment later, I could more easily make out shapes. The wolf darted down the street ahead of me. My head swam from the drink.

Foolish, foolish, foolish girl. Never again.

I grabbed my pistol. In my semi-inebriated state, if I carried my knife, I could very well fall on it and stab myself. All my senses in full alarm, I followed the wolf down the dark alley.

But Edinburgh wasn't London.

53

Using the airship towers and Edinburgh castle on the hill as my benchmarks, I tried to keep my direction but quickly lost my way. Suddenly, I found myself at a juncture deep in the alleyways. I had no idea where I was, and I couldn't see the castle anymore. Dimly lit streets trailed off in the cardinal directions. And in each alley, I spotted shadowed shapes.

Hell's bells.

The wolf had led me into a dark district. All around me, I sensed the preternatural—and not just were-wolves. Such places existed in London as well. Unless there was trouble, we Red Capes rarely entered such zones. If there was trouble, the alpha or other group leaders—such as they were—would handle it. Humans were *persona non grata* in such places. Maybe I could have gotten away with wandering through such a place in London without getting murdered due to my alliance with Lionheart—and the fact that I wore Fenton as an accessory—but I wasn't in London anymore.

I skidded to a stop. My heart thundered in my chest. I watched as shadows moved down the alleyway toward me. My head swam. Inhaling deeply, I began to slowly back away only to trip over something massive and metal. Jutting sideways, I fell to the cobblestone, scraping my lip in the process.

I turned, my gun poised, to find a hulking metal creature with glowing yellow optics looking down at me. Standing beside it was a small, stoutly built man. He swore at me in a language I didn't understand. He then activated the device in his hand. The hulking metallic creature lurked. The man and his monstrous automaton moved off into the darkness.

As I gazed down the alley, I spied ruby red eyes in the far distance. Much to my frustration, the image before me swam drunkenly. *Foolish girl.*

"Agent Louvel?" a voice said, a hand reaching down toward me. "Are ye tryin' to die?"

I looked up to see the kelpie, Eideard, standing there. Taking his hand, I rose.

Eideard cast a glance down the alley.

"Looks like ye found yer wolves. But I suggest ye go that way," he said, motioning behind us. "Even the Shadow Watch be not comin' here."

"I… Thank you."

He nodded.

I turned and looked back down the alley. The red eyes had retreated.

Damned wolves.

"Thanks again," I told Eideard. "Watch yourself," I said, eyeing the alley.

Eideard laughed. "Wee babes, these. But now ye owe me a drink."

"Agreed," I said. I smiled at him in thanks then turned and hurried out of the alley.

All right.

Okay.

Well, I had almost gotten myself murdered, but now I knew a few things. I confirmed the name of the airship —the *Fenrir*—and got a good look at Captain Zayde Skollson. I also learned a little of his intentions—to rule the skies. Very well. We'd be nipping that in the bud.

I also learned that there was at least one friendly preternatural in the city. But it seemed that Edinburgh was more ripe with problems than Shadow Watch let on. The taste of blood in my mouth and the throbbing of my sore, broken lip were also very poignant reminders that I wasn't in London anymore. And that I had no business drinking more than three stouts while on duty. Or, at least, no more than two stouts but no Scotch. Or one Scotch and one stout. Ugh.

Now I just had to make sure that my drunken mishap hadn't put my partner in danger. If I wanted to make a good impression on Edwin Hunter, it certainly wouldn't do to get my new partner murdered on her first day on the job.

Edwin.

That was a nice name.

A smile danced across my lips followed by stinging pain. I rubbed the back of my hand across my broken lip, smearing blood on my skin. *Good job, Clemeny.*

I headed back to Holyrood House Inn, which was

reassuringly quiet. Moving quickly, I went to Agent Harper's room. The door was still locked.

I knocked heavily.

There was a rustle inside. I couldn't tell if it was a good rustle or a bad rustle.

I knocked again.

More rustling but no answer.

I stepped back, preparing to bust down the door when the door suddenly opened.

On the other side, looking decidedly bedraggled, was Agent Harper.

"Clemeny? Did I oversleep?" she asked with a yawn. "Your lip is bleeding. What happened?" she asked as she pulled a dainty lace-trimmed handkerchief from her pocket. She handed it to me.

I pressed the heavily perfumed fabric against my lip.

"Get dressed. I'll tell you along the way."

"Along the way? To where?"

"To Shadow Watch."

CHAPTER 8

Shadow Watch

I sipped a cup of tea in the front parlor of the inn, trying to get my wits together, as I waited for Harper to get ready. What was it that Fenton had once said to me? That I was either really brave or really stupid? Yeah, perhaps that old werewolf was right after all. If not for the kelpie, I would have been in trouble. I'd have to remember to make good on my promise to buy that old stallion a drink. Of course, that would mean I would have to go back to the pub. Sounded like a good idea a few hours ago. Now, running the risk of ruining my reputation with my new boss by botching a job because I got tipsy flirting with a tapster seemed a lot less shiny and bright. I didn't want Agent Hunter to see me like that. That wasn't who I was. And I should have known better.

Quinn would have known better. He would have

been there to kick my ass when I did something stupid like that, or at least watch my back after the fact.

Now I had Harper, who had been in bed asleep while I was out working the case.

Fabulous.

I sighed and sipped my tea. I couldn't blame her. What did she know? She'd only ever worked in administration. This was her first case.

"Ready," Agent Harper said as she stuffed papers into her satchel as she joined me.

"What's that?" I asked, eyeing up the documents.

"Just some notes. I was trying to triangulate the pirate attacks, see if I could figure out the location of their home base. I think I have it narrowed down. Let's see if Shadow Watch will take us aloft for a look."

Impressed, I nodded. "Well done."

Agent Harper beamed a smile at me. "Thanks, Clemeny."

Harper and I headed outside.

Checking my gun, I held it in hand as we headed down the street toward Edinburgh Castle. To my surprise, the weapon didn't attract even a little attention. I kept an eye out as we moved. My head was coming back to rights after a spot of Earl Grey. Thus far, no tingly palms.

"So, I met the captain of the airship *Fenrir*," I told Harper.

Agent Harper stopped in her tracks. "You found him?"

"He found me, more like."

"Did he…" She pointed to my lip.

I laughed. "No. I tripped over the foot of an automaton being led by a dwarf."

"Dwarf? No. Would have to be a gnome."

"A gnome?"

"Little people of the hollow hills. They've been emerging, drawn by all the new technology. It seems their minds are quite sharp for it. Scary buggers in their true form, from what I've heard. They're shifters. They appear human, but their true form is not remotely as cute. Did you actually see the creature?"

"Um. No. I did not."

"And what about the werewolf? What did he say?"

"Bravado, bravado, bravado, death threat. Then tried to lead me into a trap in a dark district."

"A dark district?" Harper replied, a nervous tremor in her voice.

"That's okay. My white horse arrived in time to save me."

"Who? Also, I think the saying is *a knight on a white horse*."

"So it is, but I mean a white horse. Literally. A kelpie stepped in."

"Oh. That's…unexpected."

"Anyway, this airship pirate thinks he's the alpha of the aether, which was a new one for me. He's either Norwegian or from one of the remote Scottish isles."

"That fits with what Lionheart told you."

I nodded. "Let's see what Shadow Watch has to say, shall we?"

Harper nodded. "This way," she said.

I knew that the Shadow Watch headquarters were located in Edinburgh Castle, so I was surprised when Agent Harper led me not toward the castle itself, but around its mountain base. Glancing back and forth from a note in her hand toward the rocky crag on which the castle sat, she led us to a single gaslamp at a jumble of rocks that remotely resembled a rough-cut stairwell in the cliffside. There, I noted the letters R. M. carved into the stones.

I scanned around, trying to sense anything nearby. I activated my night optic. There wasn't anyone nearby.

"This way. Watch your step," she said.

We headed up the cliff.

Feeling very grateful once more for Master Hart's invention which showed the outline of the pseudo steps carved into the rock, I followed Agent Harper. We moved around a few jutting boulders and into a narrow pass. Ahead of us, we finally came across a very small, round metal door. It looked like the outlet for some kind of pipe. There was a wheel on the door, but when I grabbed it, it was stuck in place. I knocked on the thick panel. There was a hollow echo on the other side. The door had to have been several inches thick.

"It's a false door," Agent Harper said. Reaching into her pocket, she pulled out a thin piece of metal. Under the moonlight, I could see that the metal had been punched with an elaborate array of holes. She eyed the round door. Noting a nearly invisible slot on the side of the door, she slipped the metal card inside.

Harper motioned for me to step back.

From somewhere inside, I heard a series of gears clang, and a moment later, the hatch opened. The metal card Agent Harper used popped out. Grinning, she took it, slid it back into her vest, and then motioned for me to follow her inside.

We entered the narrow passage. It was so low that I had to duck to follow Agent Harper.

Harper pulled a lever on the wall. The metal hatch closed behind us. The metal locks tumbled back into place. The door had locked itself once more. Everything went dark.

"Damn," Agent Harper swore. "I thought a lamp would come on. You go on. You can see better with your optic."

Groaning, I scooted around Agent Harper then headed down the narrow tunnel. "You know, I'm very sure they have a front entrance. This seems immensely impractical. Who gave you instructions on how to enter?"

"Someone named Agent Walsh."

"And did you tell them you were working the case with me?"

"I… I'm not sure."

I sighed. Some senior agents enjoyed messing with the rookies. When I first started, either Quinn stepped in or the other agents just decided I wasn't a mark, but no one ever bothered me. But this was precisely the kind of prank I'd expect. And given Shadow Watch and the Red Capes had an ongoing rivalry, I suddenly had the feeling I was prey to a Scottish ruse. "All right. And where does this tunnel lead?"

"Keep an eye out for a ladder."

"Good thing I have *an* eye."

"Oh, Clemeny. I'm sorr—"

"Just kidding," I said with a laugh then headed forward. "Seriously, they must have a front door. Next time, let me do the talking."

"You think they were just messing with me?"

"Most definitely, yes."

Harper harrumphed but didn't say anything else.

Trying not to grumble under my breath, and bent in half, a position which my ginger-infused, stout-filled stomach did not enjoy, I worked my way forward. Sure enough, the narrow stone passage soon came to an abrupt end. There was a massive cavern before me and no way down.

"Um, the cliff of doom here," I said.

"Look for a ladder on the cliff wall."

I looked over the ledge. There, metal rungs had been worked into the cavern wall. I cast my gaze down. It was...far.

Sighing, I slid onto my belly then grabbed the first rung. "It's a climb," I told Agent Harper. "And whomever Agent Walsh is, I am already planning to do very, very bad things to him."

"Clemeny..."

"Don't. Say. Anything," I said, but I had to chuckle. It was a good prank, but very evil at the same time.

As Harper and I climbed down, soft music came to my ears. I distinctly made out the sound of a pipe. The ghostly tune resonated throughout the cavern.

"The piper," Agent Harper said.

"Piper?"

"Yeah, haven't you ever heard the story of the piper of Edinburgh Castle? A young boy found the caverns underneath the castle. He went in to map them, playing a pipe as he went so people above ground could hear him. But then his piping mysteriously stopped."

"So, you're saying that's the sound of a ghost I'm hearing?"

"No, Shadow Watch has a paleophone playing in the

tunnels under the castle. It scares away anyone who gets too curious."

"Splendid."

"Their headquarters really are under the castle in the bedrock. I swear. That's why I didn't question the entrance instructions. I'm sorry, Clemeny."

I chuckled. "Don't worry. It's not you I'm annoyed with."

After a climb, we reached the cavern floor. I was surprised to see the flicker of a gaslamp in a narrow passage. Due to the way the tunnel bent, I hadn't noticed the passage from above.

"There?" I asked Agent Harper.

She nodded.

We headed across the cave and into the illuminated tunnel. Gaslamps lit the path. We wound through the darkness until we met with another metal door. Agent Harper pulled out another metal card, this one a bit larger, and slipped it into a slot.

We heard a chime on the other side.

After a few minutes, the metal door opened to reveal a wooden entryway that looked much like a formal waiting room. To my surprise, a woman sat at a desk working busily on some paperwork. She looked up at us.

"Names?" she asked primly.

"Agents Harper and Louvel, Red Cape Society.

We're here to meet Agent Walsh," Harper said.

The woman's lips twitched as she suppressed a smirk.

I gave Harper a knowing glance.

She winced.

The woman pulled out a clipboard and ran her finger along the paper thereon. She nodded to us. "Very good," she said then pulled a lever on the ground beside her.

My legs shook as the room suddenly jerked. A moment later, the entire room spun on its axis, a move my ginger- and stout-filled stomach seriously disliked. A moment later, the room turned to reveal the underground headquarters of the Shadow Watch.

CHAPTER 9
Castle Rock

"Welcome to Castle Rock," the attendant said, waving for us to step into the room.

Stretched out before us was a massive workroom. Agents in their black and silver kilts worked at their desks or moved quickly to and from the offices off the main room. There was a spiral staircase at the center of the room, wide enough for four people, which extended beyond the ceiling of volcanic rock overhead. Agents hurried up and down the steps.

I pulled off my night optic and slipped on my eyepatch before anyone else had a chance to see me.

A squat man with broad shoulders, a bald head, and a massive mustache over a neatly trimmed beard crossed the room to greet us.

"Agent Harper?"

Harper nodded and stuck out her hand. "That's me."

"I'm Agent Walsh," he said, shaking her hand.

"Ah, Agent Walsh. Junior Agent Harper told me it's you we should thank for the instructions on how to enter Shadow Watch. Thank you for that."

Agent Walsh smiled at me, his grin wide and toothy. "Agent Louvel. I only just learned Harper was accompanying you. It's a pleasure to finally meet you," he said then shook my hand. His grip was firm, but his expression was playful.

"Indeed," I replied, giving his firm handshake an extra hard squeeze.

Agent Walsh laughed as he eyed the pelt on my belt. "Rumor is true then? I tangled with Fenton once. Nice to see he learned to mind his place."

"All tricksters do in time," I said, passing Agent Walsh a wink.

Agent Walsh grinned then let me go. "I'll keep that in mind. Granted, I didn't know who Harper was coming with when I sent along the, um, instructions. Now, this way, agents. Agent MacGregor is expecting you," he said then led us toward the stairwell.

As I glanced around the room, I noticed that Shadow Watch's headquarters were roughly half the size of that of the Red Cape Society. But the agents themselves struck me as looking more like battle-hardened warriors. It made sense. Shadow Watch tangled with some of the worst preternaturals in the land. Demons and other nasty buggers had a tendency to pop up beyond Hadrian's Wall. And from what I'd heard, Agent Edwin Hunter was the most feared demon hunter in the realm.

Agent Walsh led us up the spiral staircase to the second floor. We emerged in what appeared to be the lower level of Edinburgh Castle. The walls and floors were covered in hardwood. Agent Walsh led us down a hallway to a door labeled with Agent MacGregor's— Shadow Watch's lead agent—name. This was the position Agent Hunter had previously held.

Agent Walsh knocked on the door. "Sir, Red Capes are here."

"Come," a voice called.

Agent Walsh entered, motioning for us to follow along behind him.

Agent McGregor rose to greet us. He was a tall man with thinning black hair and a hawkish expression. His eyes were an icy blue color. I gazed around the room. It hadn't taken long for him to redecorate. The coat of arms for Clan MacGregor, paintings of ancestral castles, and a large portrait of Rob Roy MacGregor hung on the walls.

"Agent Harper and Agent Louvel," Agent MacGregor said, looking from one to the other of us in turn, his eyes briefly scanning the eyepatch on my face. He motioned for us to sit. "So, what can you tell me about the menace I've got overhead?"

I sunk into the seat. "The airship *Fenrir*," I said.

Agent MacGregor folded his fingers into a steeple and bobbed them gently against his lips.

"Wolves, of course. Painting themselves as Vikings. Managed to meet their captain a few hours back. Hulking beast, blond, lots of tattoos, very Norse. His name is Zayde Skollson."

"Airship Vikings?" Agent Walsh said in surprise. "That's a first. These days, nobody expects a Viking invasion."

"No, they do not," I concurred with a soft chuckle. "Apparently Zayde Skollson fancies himself the alpha of the aether."

Agent MacGregor exhaled slowly as he considered.

"Sir, if Shadow Watch would be kind enough to take Agent Louvel and me back up, I have triangulated the airship *Fenrir's* movements, and I believe—" Harper began.

"You encountered the airship captain. Here? In the city?" Agent MacGregor asked, cutting Harper short as he turned to me.

I stilled. Maybe it was the crawl through the tunnel or the post-stout headache that was forming, but the slight to Harper agitated me. I turned to my partner.

"As Agent Harper was saying, she has triangulated the airship *Fenrir's* movements. Once we go back up, we know where to hunt him."

"I see," Agent MacGregor answered. He kept his gaze firm, but it was clear he had not missed my cue. "We'll make the arrangements for that. Very good, Agent Harper."

"And yes, I did meet Zayde Skollson in the city. As one expects, he threatened my life, lured me into a dark district, then loped off. Typical posturing. All it means is that he's nervous. And he should be. Agent Harper has leveraged us an advantage."

"Yes. Well. I'm just surprised the scoundrel showed up here in the city. Agent Harper, where have you placed him?"

Agent Harper pulled out her map. "May I set this out?" she asked.

Agent MacGregor motioned for her to use a round worktable in the corner. Rising, we followed Harper as she laid out her map. "You see, I have noted the locations of the attacks. It seems that wherever their base is, it can't be far from this area. They're hunting the trade routes, but only within this circumference," she said, noting a circle she's drawn on the map.

I looked at the map. "What's this?" I asked, pointing to a tiny green spot amongst the blue.

"Fair Isle," Agent Walsh said. "In the Shetlands."

"Isn't that where the airship crew you interviewed in London spotted her?"

Agent Harper nodded. "We should scout this area."

Agent MacGregor nodded. "Let's see what we can find," he said then turned to Agent Walsh. "Ask Captain Martin to take her up again. This time, more guns."

"Yes, sir."

"And Agent Louvel, do be careful poking around Edinburgh. Our dark district is a bit unsettled at the moment. Some shifts of power taking place. I believe you just went through the same kind of commotion in London."

"Yes, sir. With the werewolves' alpha."

Agent MacGregor nodded. "I wish werewolves were our only problem."

"Seems you do have a unique set of preternaturals in Scotland. I met my first kelpie tonight."

Both Agent Walsh and Agent MacGregor became deathly still.

"What did you say?" Agent Walsh asked.

"I...I said I met a kelpie."

"A kelpie? Where?"

"I met him at a pub. In fact, he saved my arse from a patch of trouble."

Both looking astonished, the two agents looked from one another to me.

"He said his name was Eideard," I added.

"And he lent you a hand? Did he know who you were?"

"Yes, he did. In fact, he bought me a drink at the pub. Though I think he was just trying to make sure I left him alone. Ran across him again in the dark district. The wolves didn't seem very interested in tangling with him. Why? What's the problem?"

Agent MacGregor shook his head in astonishment. "You, Agent Louvel, are fortunate to be alive."

"But he's just a shifter."

"That he is, when he isn't busy paddling around Loch Ness," Agent MacGregor said then turned to Agent Walsh. "Let Ailith know her boy was spotted in the city. She needs to get him rounded up and headed back home before he upsets the balance of things worse than they already are. Christ, Eideard. Why now of all times?"

"From what I saw, it looked like he had an itch to scratch," I said with a slight grin.

Catching my meaning, Agent Walsh chuckled. "That would do it. I'll let Agent Monroe know, sir," he told his boss.

Agent MacGregor nodded. "Very good, Agents. Agent Walsh will see to it you are aloft by tomorrow. Please let us know if you need anything else," Agent MacGregor said then went back to his desk.

"This way," Agent Walsh said then led us back into the main room. We went to a lift on the far side of the room. Once we stepped inside, Agent Walsh activated a lever, and the wooden wall panels closed behind us.

"Agent Walsh, are you telling us that Agent Louvel met the Loch Ness monster?" Agent Harper asked, unable to hide the astonishment in her voice.

Agent Walsh chuckled. "Indeed she did. Old Eideard is the oldest cryptid in the realm and stronger than any werewolf alive. And he *hates* us. Must have been something about you he liked, Agent Louvel," he said then gave me a curious look. "Otherwise, you'd be dead. Lucky."

When the lift came to a stop, it chimed, and the doors opened to reveal a narrow passageway which, from the look of the stone walls, carpets, and oil paintings, was on an upper floor of Edinburgh Castle. A well-armed castle guard stood waiting.

"See them out, George," Agent Walsh told the guard standing there then turned to us. "Expect someone at the inn tomorrow. I'll make the arrangements. And Agent Louvel, try not to unbalance the entire preternatural society in Scotland in a single night," he said with a wink then tugged on a lever, closing the lift door behind him.

"This way, Agents," the guard said.

"What was that about?" Agent Harper whispered to me.

"Which part?"

"You know, the bit about the shifts of power, the unbalanced society, and the... waterhorse. I thought they were going to faint," she said then laughed.

I smirked. "So did I."

Agent Harper shook her head. "First Lionheart and now that creature. You certainly have a way with them, Clemeny. I wonder why."

"Like Walsh said. Luck, I guess."

"Hmm," Agent Harper mused.

I frowned. Eideard hadn't seemed that bad. Wary, yes. Dangerous, perhaps. But hateful? Not to me, at least. Maybe it was the way I thought about the preternaturals that set me apart. I didn't know about Eideard, but Sir Richard Spencer had once been human. Most of the preternaturals were, after all, just people. Just people who'd been modified. As such, they ranged from good to bad. Hell, even the vampire Constantine—wherever he'd gone—still had some of his humanity left in him.

However, I knew not all my colleagues saw them like that. Some only saw the monster. And many, like Cyril and Fenton, deserved it. But not all of them.

The guard led us through a series of hallways, behind a tapestry, through a narrow passage, across the kitchens, through a garden, and finally, to the front of Edinburgh Castle.

With a nod, he left us there.

Grinning, I looked at Agent Harper. "Told you they had a front entrance."

Rolling her eyes at me, we turned and headed back into the city. That single exasperated gesture filled my heart with hope. Maybe this partnership would work out after all.

CHAPTER 10

Ginger Brew

It was around two in the morning when we finally returned to the inn.

"I'm going to go over my notes again. Want to join me?" Agent Harper asked as she unlocked the door to her room.

"Considering I didn't have the luxury of a lengthy nap, I'll pass."

Harper scrunched up her brow. "Sorry, Clemeny. I—"

I clapped her on the shoulder. "No worries."

"Thank you. And back at Shadow Watch, when Agent MacGregor brushed me off… Thanks for that too."

I shrugged. "It was nothing. But next time, speak up. Show them the steel in your spine, and you won't be sent down a cave tunnel again."

Harper grinned at me. "Thanks, Clemeny. Goodnight."

I nodded to her. "Goodnight," I said then headed to my room.

Once inside, I went to the window and looked out. It was quiet on the street below. My sixth sense didn't feel the unseen. I watched the few stragglers still meandering up and down the street. What, exactly, was unbalanced in Scotland that had everyone so on edge? Not my beat. Not my problem.

Pulling off my cloak, I tossed it on the corner of my bed then sat down at the dressing table. I looked in the mirror. Leaning in, I inspected my split lip. The wound had sealed, but the lip was puffy and discolored. I pulled off my eyepatch and set it on the table. Sitting back, I took a long look at myself. I wasn't sure how, but when Fenton had scratched me, he had also damaged the roots of my hair. My previously black hair was now streaked white. Three long scars went from my hairline, across my face, and onto my cheek.

I looked at my mooneye. There was no color left, just white. I was lucky that I could still see something, even if it was only shadows. But still. The truth was, I'd been disfigured. The girl in the mirror, one I barely recognized as myself, was a mess.

Sighing, I rose and went to the bed. Pulling off my silver vambraces, I lay down. My head on my pillow, my dagger in one hand and a pistol in the other, I willed myself to sleep, reminding myself that I'd be aloft tomorrow once more.

And I was almost out of candied ginger.

IT WAS STILL EARLY WHEN CAPTAIN MARTIN ARRIVED THE next morning. The fog had barely lifted off the streets and the lamplighters were working their way down the Royal Mile.

Reluctantly, I got myself ready then joined Agent Harper and Captain Martin who were already waiting downstairs.

"G'morning, Agents. We're docked at the towers," Captain Martin said, motioning to the Edinburgh Towers. "Ah, Agent Louvel, I have something for you. My wife sent it along."

"Your wife, sir?"

Captain Martin smiled. "I told my wife I finally met someone who gets more airsick than her. When she heard I was taking you back up, she told me to bring you this," he said, handing me a flask.

I took it. "What is it?"

"Well, I don't know for sure, but I do know my house smelled like mint and ginger while it was brewing. The cat sneezed all night long. She said to tell you to sip it as needed."

I chuckled. "Please give your wife my thanks."

He nodded.

As we walked, I opened the lid on the flask and gave it a sniff. The strong scents of ginger, mint, and other herbs assailed my nose, making me wince. I took a small sip. The concoction was so strong my sinuses cleared at once.

I pushed the flask toward Harper. She lifted it and took a sniff. Handing it back, she shook her head no so violently I thought she might hurt herself.

Once we arrived at the airship towers, we took the lift up. Maybe it was just the anticipation of being aloft once more, but I could already feel the unsteady sway as we made our way down the platform toward the *Jacobite*. When we climbed aboard the airship, it became clear that Agent MacGregor's request for more guns had been heard loud and clear. This time, it seemed, we were travelling with a small army.

I grinned, wondering what Quinn would think about this turn of events. No doubt, he would have complained about them getting in the way. But Quinn never had to chase werewolves through the sky before.

Agent Harper went to the wheelstand and spoke to Captain Martin. Not long afterward, the airship lifted out of port and headed north.

I found a spot near the prow of the ship. Hanging on to a rope, I tried to reassure my stomach that Mrs. Martin's brew was going to work wonders.

"We're headed toward Fair Isle," Harper said when she joined me.

"Good."

"Clemeny... What will we do if we find them? I mean, what did you and Quinn usually do?"

"We arrested them if we could."

"And if you...if *we* can't?"

"And if we can't?" I patted the pelt on my belt. "What do you say, Fenton?"

Agent Harper laughed nervously but didn't say anything else. I had a feeling that very soon I'd see what Harper was made of.

CHAPTER 11

Dogfights

C aptain Martin took us up into the clouds. The ride north was uneventful, but when we finally passed over the shore and began flying above the waters north of Scotland, an uneasiness washed over me. And it wasn't my stomach talking.

My sixth sense came alive.

They were there. Somewhere.

Keeping us hidden amongst the clouds, Captain Martin cruised into the area frequented by the airship *Fenrir*. The massive airship *Jacobite* had three propellers, one on each side and one below. The captain instructed his crew to run with only the lower propeller going. It cut the noise significantly. We drifted through the clouds, watching and waiting.

I stared out into the dense cloudbank.

We cruised around slowly, Harper using her map as

a guide. She'd already identified the most popular shipping and trade routes north. The Viking ship had been lingering around the edges, looking for anyone on which to prey.

In the distance, I saw a shadow of another ship moving through the clouds.

I snapped my fingers and pointed.

The captain lifted his spyglass. I pulled out my tinkered optic and slid it on. Dropping down the magnification lens, I looked out.

It wasn't him.

I looked back toward Captain Martin who shook his head, confirming my assessment.

A moment later, a raven appeared from somewhere deep within the cloudbank. It circled around the *Jacobite*. Alighting on a rope, it cawed then flew off in the direction of the other airship. Soon, other black-winged birds appeared, following the first to the vessel off the starboard side. The entire unkindness of birds circled the other airship.

A sick feeling knotted my stomach. I switched my lens on my optic into night vision mode and looked all around.

The palms of my hands itched.

There, moving slowing under the cloud cover, I spied the shadow of a massive wolf head at the prow of an airship. And onboard, glowing red eyes. But they weren't watching us. I wasn't even sure if they'd seen us at all. They were moving in slowly, propelled by momentum, toward the second ship. It was like watching a predator stalk its prey.

"Hell's bells." I turned and ran back to the captain.

The entire crew turned to watch me.

"There," I whispered, pointing toward the dense clouds. "They're hiding in there."

Harper followed my gaze, squinting to look.

The captain lifted his spyglass. "Like shadows," he whispered then a moment later, he signaled to his crew.

The men readied their guns. Crewmen rushed belowdecks.

There was a click as the second and third gears in the galley turned on.

Captain Martin motioned to the balloonman.

Hot air hissed as the balloon filled. The airship lifted quickly, my stomach flipping along with it.

The *Jacobite* rose out of sight moments before the airship *Fenrir* launched her attack on the unsuspecting merchant vessel. There were shouts and screams as the Viking warship attacked. Through the misty air, I could hear Skollson barking orders. The merchant ship picked up speed as it tried to escape, the *Fenrir* racing up alongside her. Damn, that ship was fast.

The *Jacobite* turned slowly.

"Ready the guns," Captain Martin called.

The *Jacobite* turned, aligning herself with the other ships.

The captain grabbed the rope that led to the signal in the gear galley.

"Now," Captain Martin called to his crew, yanking on the line. Below, a bell rang. A moment later, the *Jacobite* shot off in the direction of the *Fenrir* and her prey, the *Jacobite's* guns at the ready. The captain steered us toward the confrontation.

Orange gunsmoke lit up the clouds as the airship *Fenrir* attacked the merchant vessel. Captain Martin sped toward them, but we were still hiding aloft. Once we neared the fray, Captain Martin motioned to the balloonman who yanked open the flap at the top of the balloon. The airship quickly started to sink.

Grabbing on to a rope, I inhaled deeply as my stomach heaved. With many, many blessings heaped on Captain Martin's wife, the contents of my stomach stayed in my stomach.

Once again, a raven flew near our ship.

This time, however, it cawed loudly. The entire unkindness of birds headed toward us.

Steadying myself, I rushed to the front of the ship. The merchant vessel was moving fast, trying to outrun the *Fenrir*, but the Viking ship had already pulled up alongside her and was edging in to tether to the second ship.

When the *Jacobite* descended from the clouds, I heard shouting from the *Fenrir.*

A moment later, Zayde Skollson appeared at the stern.

Standing at the front of the ship, my red cape swirling around me, I waved to him.

The werewolf's eyes flashed red.

He shouted something over his shoulder, and at once, the Viking ship began to disengage. Looking angry, he turned and stalked back onto the deck of his ship and out of sight.

"Starboard side. Guns ready," Captain Martin shouted.

As the *Jacobite* approached the *Fenrir*, the Viking ship turned in an effort to make a hasty getaway.

"Fire," Captain Martin shouted.

Guns blasting, I heard the wood on the gondola of the airship *Fenrir* crack. Moving quickly, the airship turned and headed back toward the cover of the thick clouds. The propeller at the back of the Viking airship came up to speed, and a moment later, the airship sped away from the *Jacobite's* assault.

Captain Martin began to make chase. "Speed. We need more speed," he called to the gear galley.

Two men toting long-range guns raced toward the front of the airship and continued the barrage.

Despite the fact that the gears below were turning

rapidly, we quickly lost pace. I watched as the *Fenrir* slowly disappeared back into the clouds.

"Dammit! We're losing him. More speed," Captain Martin barked.

The *Jacobite* lurched then moved ahead.

But not quickly enough.

The lightweight *Fenrir*, far more agile than the hulking *Jacobite*, disappeared.

As it did, the ravens followed along behind it.

"They're using the bloody birds as scouts," I said, turning to Agent Harper who nodded.

"Clever pirates," one of the crewmen standing nearby grumbled.

"Not pirates. Vikings," Harper said with a smirk.

Clever, clever Vikings.

WE SPENT THE REST OF THE DAY HUNTING THE *FENRIR*, BUT it was no use. The airship had retreated.

"Take Harper and me to the port at Thurso," I told Captain Martin. "We'll go by sea to Fair Isle."

"By sea?"

I nodded. "The *Jacobite* can head back to Edinburgh. We'll return to the city tomorrow or the day after."

"But Agent Louvel—"

"No offense, Captain Martin. You've done all you

could here. The *Fenrir* is too fast for the *Jacobite*. I'll flush him out my way."

"Of course, Agent," Captain Martin said, and the airship turned, heading back toward land.

"You have an idea?" Agent Harper asked me.

I nodded. "He knows we're looking for him aloft. So, let's go find him where he isn't expecting us."

"On the ground?"

"You got it."

"And then?"

"And then… Well, we'll see."

CHAPTER 12

Thurso

The airship port at Thurso was rudimentary, to say the least. The northern village had been occupied since the days Thorfinn the Mighty terrorized the seas. Today, it was filled with fishermen, villagers, and drunks.

But the local pub was always the best place to find gossip and a charter. To our luck—or was it a detriment? From the smell I wasn't sure—there was a pub not far from the airship tower where the *Jacobite* had left us.

"Come on," I told Harper, leading her to The Salty Mermaid which sat on the cart path between the airship towers and the seaport. Thurso was decidedly unmodernized. It might as well have been the eighteenth century here.

We headed inside The Salty Mermaid. Grabbing a

table that had a good view of both the back door and the front, Harper and I slid into our seats.

The barkeep whistled at a girl who'd been washing cups, motioning for her to wait on us.

"Ale, misses?" the young girl, who was about twelve or so, asked.

"What do you have to eat?" I asked.

"Fish and chips. Kidney pie. Plowman's platters."

"Fish and chips," Harper said.

"Same," I added.

"And two stouts?" Harper said, looking at me.

I shook my head. "No, no, no. Have tea?"

"No, but I have water," the girl said.

"Water it will be then. One stout, one water."

The girl nodded then headed back.

I cast a glance around the room. Fishermen, airship crews, and other workers filled the busy pub. Suddenly, I wished I had Lionheart's ears.

"Always take a seat where you can see the exits," I told Harper. "Don't just watch who is already in the room, keep an eye on who is coming, going, and how you can get the hell out in a hurry."

"Front door. Back exit," Harper said, motioning with her chin.

"And?"

"I... I don't know."

I motioned to the window. "There's always a way

out if you really need one. Did they give you a gun?"

She nodded then tapped the satchel she always wore strung around her body bandolier style.

"Take it out. Wear it on your belt. If you need to pull it in a hurry, you won't have time to drag it out of your reticule," I said with a wink.

"Hey, this isn't a reticule. It's a journeyman's satchel. And it was a gift."

"It's a very nice satchel, I don't disagree. But not for carrying a weapon," I said then eyed the leather bag more closely. Someone had taken great care to purchase the bag for Harper. The initials E. H. surrounded by a nice filigree were burned into the leather. "Harper, what's your first name?"

"Elaine."

I nodded. "Elaine."

"And who, Elaine, gave you such a nice satchel?"

Harper shifted nervously. "A friend…at the Society."

The barmaiden returned with the drinks. Harper snatched hers straight away, relieved to find an excuse not to talk more. But now my curiosity was piqued. I leaned back in my seat and sipped my water. I didn't remember Harper ever spending time with any of the male agents. Well, except for Agent Hunter. The idea that Hunter was the mysterious gift giver suddenly made me feel very jealous. I looked at the satchel once more. It *was* relatively new. I frowned.

"Did you ever meet Allan Quartermain?" Agent Harper asked, her voice light and a little nervous.

Allan Quartermain, who had a reputation as a big game hunter and royalist, was frequently in Africa on behest of Her Majesty. And unbeknownst to most, it wasn't lions Quartermain was hunting. He was head of the small division that dealt with the preternaturals in the colonies, a job I would wish on no one. But the young agent had a keen eye and good sense for the job. I'd never been introduced to him, but I'd seen him once or twice while he was in the office before heading back out to the field.

"No, but I know him by reputation."

"We're childhood friends," Harper replied. "He gave me the satchel before he left for Africa again," she said then sipped her drink.

There was a tinge of sadness in her voice. I sensed a lot of unspoken story there, and despite my curiosity, one that didn't need me digging around into it.

I smiled. "Well, it's a nice bag, but put your gun on your belt. Quartermain would never forgive me if I let you get shot. And something tells me I don't want a man who can shoot me from two miles away on my bad side."

At that, Harper laughed then pulled out her pistol and slipped it into her holster.

Once again, the girl returned. This time, she had two

heaping plates loaded with fried fish and chips. My stomach growled hungrily at the sight. Rising, I took the plate from the girl's hand, popping a burning hot chip as I sat back down. "Thank you," I told her through bites. Despite the pain, the lure of salt, oil, and potatoes was too much to deny. I took another bite, burning my tongue in the process.

Harper looked at me, smirking as she gently laid her napkin across her lap.

Seems I'd been working with Quinn far too long. But then again, Quinn also had better table manners than me, despite Grand-mere's repeated attempts to teach me.

"What? I'm hungry," I said, grabbing another chip. The tavern girl chuckled.

"You're going to burn your fingers," Harper told me then lifted her fork and knife.

"Already burned my tongue," I said with a laugh then grabbed my fork.

"Anything else, misses?" the girl asked.

Harper shook her head.

"We need a ferry. Who do you think would talk to us?" I asked the girl.

She looked over her shoulder, scanning the room. "In the corner by the cabinet. Try them. Let me know if you need anything else," she said then headed back behind the bar.

I noted the table the girl had mentioned. There, an ancient man and woman sat nursing their cups. Both looked half-asleep, and from their clothes, very hard up. The girl's instincts were right. The other men in the room would gossip, ask questions, or be too paranoid to take us anywhere. The old couple? They looked like they could use the coin.

I turned back to my food, scarfing it down as quickly as I could. The batter in which the fish had been cooked had pools of hot oil that burned my mouth, but the pain was so worth it. Grand-mère had raised me with a snobbish love of French cuisine, but nothing could shake my taste for salty and oily pub food.

Once I was done, I looked at Harper who still had half her plate.

She stared at me.

I winked, washed the meal down with my water, then crossed the room to talk to the old man and woman. I pulled up a seat beside their table, the legs on the chair squeaking. They both looked up at me.

"My partner and I are looking for a charter," I told the old couple.

They were an ancient pair. The old man had tattoos on his arms and face, but they had long since faded. The old woman had long silver hair and light-colored eyes. There was something decidedly unusual about them. They were human, kind of. Maybe it was the glow of the otherworld on them, the nearness of death, or perhaps it was something else, but they were *off*.

"To where?" the man asked. His accent was so thick, I could barely make out his words.

"Fair Isle," I said in a soft voice so the nosey barman wouldn't hear.

"Lots of isles hereabout. You sure you want that one?" the woman asked. To my surprise, she smirked at me.

"Do you have a better suggestion?"

"I do. Probably best we don't go out now though. Too close to nightfall."

I leaned back in my seat and folded my arms across my chest.

"Really?"

The old woman winked at the man sitting across from her. "The ravens tell me North Ronaldsay would suit better. Wouldn't you say, love?"

"Oh, aye."

I looked from the man to the woman. I grinned. "All right. Shall I meet you at the port in the morning then?"

"Aye," the woman said.

"Aye," her companion agreed.

"Your ship's name?"

"The *Boudicca*," the woman replied.

"Very well. Thank you," I said then rose.

Odd. Definitely odd.

MELANIE KARSAK

I turned and motioned to Harper that it was time to go. Harper dropped some coins on the table then we headed outside.

"We'll go in the morning," I told her.

"That's fine. But where are we going to sleep tonight?"

"What, you don't have your standard issue bedroll in your fancy journeyman's satchel?"

"What? You mean to say we're going to sleep outside? Clemeny, I don't think…"

I laughed. "No, we're not. There is an inn down the way."

"Are we safe here though?"

"No," I said with a chuckle. "God knows what strange buggers are lurking about. And then there are the preternaturals."

Harper chuckled. "Oh."

I wrapped my arm good-naturedly around her shoulder. "Well, at the very least, we aren't out in the savanna hunting lions like Quartermain."

"You know those aren't really lions, right?"

"I do. And whatever bogeys he's chasing, I'm just glad it's not me."

Harper laughed. "Same."

And with that, we headed toward the dilapidated building at the edge of town aptly named The Seawolf.

CHAPTER 13

North Ronaldsay

A s soon as the sun had risen, Harper and I headed to the port where we found the old couple already waiting. With less than a dozen words spoken between us, we set sail for North Ronaldsay.

I eyed the old couple carefully. In truth, I knew little of Scottish folklore. These two were a curious pair. My palms didn't itch when I was around them, but still, there was more to them than met the eye.

"What is it?" Harper asked as she sat down along-side me.

"Probably nothing. Just wondering about them," I said, passing a glance at the couple.

"They are curious. The man's tattoos… The symbols are old. Celtic. Possibly druidic."

"But I thought the druids were hanging around Stonehenge."

"They aren't *always* hanging around Stonehenge. Have you ever been there? There's nothing there but the stones, some mounds, and a big, windy field. I haven't seen those symbols before except on standing stones."

I pulled off my eyepatch and looked at the old woman. There was a shimmer around her shape, a swirl of silver light. And around the old man, a shine of green and gold. Druids. Well, that was a new one for me.

I turned and looked at Harper.

She stared at me, her eyes on my mangled face. She swallowed a gasp.

"Yeah, bloody awful, isn't it?" I said, touching the still-tender skin.

"I didn't know… Your eye. It's a mooneye."

I nodded. "Pretty, isn't it?"

Harper gave me a sympathetic smile. "Can you see at all?"

"Silhouettes."

"I'm sorry."

I shrugged then pulled my eyepatch back on. "It's all right. He went after my grand-mère. Couldn't let that happen. I got the better of him in the end. Bloody werewolf."

To my surprise, the man and woman chuckled, but neither said anything to me. Working deftly, they guided the ship across the dark blue waves and into port at the northernmost Orcadian island.

Once the ship was tied up, Harper debarked, and I went to the couple. "Thank you," I said, handing them payment.

The woman gently pushed my hand back. "Go chase the devils out of my country, Clemeny Louvel."

"I… How did you…"

She chuckled. "Blood knows blood. Be safe."

I looked from her to the old man. He touched his fingertips to his forehead.

"Thank you," I told them.

The woman nodded.

Once I debarked, the pair unlashed the ship then set sail once more, guiding the vessel back out to sea.

I headed down the dock and joined Harper. What did she mean, *blood knows blood*? What kind of blood? Was she talking about the druids? What did I have to do with the druids?

Frowning, I joined Harper who waited for me at the end of the pier.

"Okay, now what?" she asked.

"Well, first, how big is North Ronaldsay?"

"Oh, a couple miles around, I suppose."

"Population?"

"Less than one hundred, maybe?"

I nodded. "Won't take long then."

"Long to do what?"

"To find out if there is anything weird happening here."

"Aside from the mysterious ship *Boudicca*?" Harper asked, looking back out to sea.

"Yeah, aside from that."

"All right. Let's go chat with the locals," Harper said then shifted her journeyman's satchel, adjusting her belt so her pistol was readily at hand.

I grinned at her. Maybe she was going to work out after all.

IT DIDN'T TAKE LONG TO "TALK TO THE LOCALS." JUST about everyone we met had a story to tell about the strange lights and noises in the caves on the far side of the island, stories of missing livestock, and the appearance of some rough looking men in the village. The crew of the airship *Fenrir*, it seemed, was doing an abysmal job of keeping a low profile.

After getting some directions, Harper and I set out to investigate. We headed across the wind-swept landscape to the western side of the island where a series of coves and caves dotted the seashore. Following the cliff, we soon spotted a cove where a single airship docking station had been built. There, the airship *Fenrir* sat tethered.

Harper and I approached the site carefully. We stayed on the cliffside above the port. It seemed that the crew was using the caves as a makeshift base from which they were launching their attacks.

"We need to stay downwind," I told Harper, lifting a few blades of grass and dropping them in the air. "They have good noses."

"Oh. Wonderful."

"Hey, you wanted to try out this beat."

"Yeah, you're right."

"And?"

"And what?"

"What do you think so far?"

Harper chuckled. "Well, no one's tried to kill me yet, which is a good sign.

"The day is still young."

She shook her head. "It's not the daytime I'm worried about."

"Smart."

We stayed low as we approached. Lying on our bellies in the grass, we surveyed the scene. Harper pulled out her spyglass while I used my magnification lens.

"It's quiet," Harper said. "Just a few people milling about the cave."

I scrunched up my right eye so I could look out the left. Everything was shadowy, but I was able to see the glow of the preternatural all around the airship. Opening my eye, I looked once more.

"There. On the ship. That's the captain, Zayde Skollson," I said.

"That blond brute?"

"Alpha in the aether."

"But alpha of how many? One ship or more? You suppose he's a lone wolf? We should contact Oslo," Harper suggested.

"Good idea. He may be a known operator."

"Could be he's trying to reclaim a dead tradition, strike out on his own. He may very well be alone," Harper said.

"I certainly hope so," I replied, suddenly dreading the thought of werewolves dropping out of the skies from all directions, an image which was both horrifying and funny all at once.

"I count twelve wolves," Harper said.

"Let's assume thirteen."

"Why?"

"Well, thirteen is unlucky, and in this job, we're always unlucky. And when don't you get a baker's dozen?"

Harper chuckled. "All right. Now what, partner?"

"Surveillance. Then we head back to Edinburgh and get Shadow Watch involved."

"The *Boudicca* left."

"There was an airship port in the village."

"You did see that airship, right? It was older than both of us together. And it only had one old prop."

"Hey, the *Stargazer* was a one-prop."

"Yeah, but it was also a racing ship."

Harper and I settled in behind the patch of rocks and kept our eyes on the *Fenrir*. The crew was busy unloading crates and barrels into the cave. Afterward, I saw the balloonman roll a pallet of fuel onto the ship. Then the gunners started loading boxes of ammo onto the ship.

"They must be heading back out," I whispered.

Harper nodded.

Through the still air, we heard the loud cawing of ravens. A swirl of black emerged from the cave.

"Hell's bells," I swore. "Forgot about the bloody birds."

"Why does it always have to be ravens? Why can't it ever be a flock of songbirds or something nice? Like a flock of butterflies?"

"Butterflies don't flock. A group of butterflies is called a kaleidoscope."

"Wait, how do you—"

"Quinn. And only princesses can conjure up a kaleidoscope of butterflies. Don't you read fairy tales?"

Harper laughed.

Frowning, I watched as the crew boarded the ship. Six stayed on the *Fenrir,* six stayed behind at the camp. I assumed the seventh was wherever would be the least convenient when the time came.

Six wasn't many. Harper and I could take the ground crew out.

But there were two problems with that plan. One, Harper wasn't Quinn. She was smart and capable, but she was still a junior agent with no field experience. And second, I didn't want the captain to know I'd discovered his whereabouts just yet.

"Um, you see that, right?" Harper whispered as she began to move back.

I followed her gaze. The *Fenrir* had lifted out of port and was turning in our direction, the unkindness of ravens not far behind.

I looked behind us. There was little more than a vast, empty field. We were painfully exposed.

I sighed. "Complications. Always complications."

"What do we do? Those birds are going to spot us."

I scanned the field. There, in the distance, was a ring of standing stones. The Dís's words, *"the old ones will always shelter,"* came back to me. I had assumed she'd meant people, old races, old preternaturals. But there was little older in the realm than the rings—except maybe Eideard. And, at least in some legends, the stones were said to have once been people.

"There. The standing stones," I said, pointing to a ring of menhir.

Staying low, Harper and I raced toward the stones. I snatched off my cape and stuffed it into my bag. Harper did the same.

The ring of stones was complete with a tomb at the center. The tomb consisted of three side stones and a massive capstone.

"There," I told Harper. "In the tomb."

The palms of my hands prickled, the bottoms of my feet itched, and my skin rose in goosebumps, but there was nowhere else to go. The minute Harper and I entered the ring of stones, I felt like my skin was on fire with energy. I ignored the sensation and raced toward the center tomb. Crouching low, Harper and I crawled inside, hiding under the shelter of the cap. It would be impossible to see us from above. As long as they didn't smell us, and those damned birds didn't investigate too carefully, this was going to work.

Harper's eyes were wide as she peered out the entrance to the tomb. She stared off into the distance, waiting for the airship to appear over the cliff ledge.

I inhaled deeply and tried to shake off the feeling of magic all around me.

We really, really needed to get out of there. It was cramped, dark, and if the raised earth beneath my feet was any indication, we were standing on the bones of someone who had once been really important. Inside a druid's tomb was no place for a living person. There was too much magic here.

A warm, soft breeze blew from the back of the tomb. It ruffled my hair. Along with it, I smelled the sweetest scent. Apple blossoms?

"Clemeny."

My heart skipped a beat.

Oh, hell's bells.

"There," Harper whispered.

The *Fenrir* rose above the cliff and disappeared into the sky, the bloody birds following along behind it.

Harper and I held our breaths as we waited for the airship to pass overhead.

"Clemeny."

I got the distinct, creepy, and wholly unexpected feeling that there was someone standing right behind me.

Harper turned her face so she could look out of the small crack in the stones overhead, watching as the airship and the birds disappeared. "They're going up," she whispered. "Headed south."

"Clemeny."

Once more, I smelled apple blossoms. There was a

softness to the air, like being in a park just after a spring rainstorm. The wind was warm and sweet.

"Okay, it's clear. They're in the clouds, and the birds are gone," Harper said then began creeping back out. "Oi, my back. Cramped in there. Clem, you coming?"

"I… Yeah." *Don't look back. Don't look back. Don't look back.*

Moving carefully, I shifted out from the under the rocks, decidedly *not* looking back, not even when someone lifted a long strand of my hair and stroked it gently as I moved away.

CHAPTER 14
The Menapii

H arper and I returned to the tiny village on North Ronaldsay where we convinced a very grouchy airship pilot—after promising a lot of coin—to give us a lift back to Thurso. The rickety old airship, which seemed like it was sewn together more by the sheer will of the captain than anything made of wood and metal, arrived in port with an exhausted huff of fishy smelling smoke from the burner basket.

Now we just needed to find a ride back to Edinburgh.

"Look," Harper said, pointing to a well-dressed airship captain talking to the Thurso stationmaster. "Belgian flag. Let's see if he's headed home."

Our red capes whipping around us, we headed down the ramp to the captain and the stationmaster.

The captain paused midsentence and gave us both a short bow.

"Ladies," the stationmaster said in surprise. "Surprised to see you here. I thought your ride left yesterday."

I frowned at him, annoyed that he'd taken notice of the *Jacobite's*—and mine and Harper's—comings and goings. But it was to be expected. In London, it was a lot easier to blend in. Here, Harper and I were like poppies in a field covered with snow. "Yes, well, needed to pop back by. Forgot my reticule."

The stationmaster snorted.

The Belgian captain smiled. Not a bad smile either, equipped with dimples on both cheeks.

I returned the expression, but then the captain's eyes drifted to Harper. And stayed there.

Oh, sure, gawk at the girl with two working eyes. Of course.

"I was wondering, if you don't mind me asking, where you are headed, sir? We need a lift to Edinburgh," Harper told the captain.

"You're in luck. I'm headed to Bruges by way of Edinburgh then London. My crew heard talk of pirating over Scotland, so we thought we'd stop for a chat, see what anyone knew. I was just planning to lift anchor."

"Pirating. Bah. Just rumors," the grizzled old stationmaster told the captain.

"Rumors? That's understating it a bit, isn't it?" I asked the man who rolled his eyes at me.

"There are reports of pirating, sir. It's true. You should stay off the trade routes," Harper told the captain, which earned her an annoyed glare from the stationmaster.

"What?" she protested indignantly. "The Viking ship *is* watching the trade lanes."

"Viking ship," the stationmaster said with a laugh. "Now, that's a good one."

I eyed the stationmaster. His dismissive attitude and reckless disregard for Harper's warning did not escape my attention.

"What does she know? She's a civilian. The wind is better if you take the shipping route south," the station-master assured the captain.

When Harper meant to protest again, I set my hand on her arm and shook my head.

"Ladies, you are welcome to join us," the captain told Harper and me—well, mostly just Harper—then turned back to the stationmaster. "Thank you for your advice, sir," the captain told him then we all turned and went to the airship which, I noted, was named *The Menapii.*

Behind us, the stationmaster grumbled then went back to his post.

Once we were aboard, I motioned to Harper and

found a spot out of the way but not far from the wheel-stand. Digging into my pocket, I pulled out the flask Captain Martin had given me. I gave it a shake. More than half left. Surprisingly, the brew worked much better than the candied ginger.

The crew untied the ship, and it lifted out of port. Once the captain had the ship aloft, Harper and I joined him.

"Stay off the shipping routes. The stationmaster lied," I told the captain. "The airship pirate is hunting along the trade routes."

"Vikings," Harper corrected.

"Sorry, airship Vikings," I said.

"Are you sure?" the captain asked.

"Yes. The stationmaster is on the take."

"How do you know?" Harper asked me.

My hands tingled. I went to the starboard side of the ship. Pulling out my pistol, I eyed the mist around us then lifted my gun.

"Clemeny?" Harper asked.

There.

I took aim then pulled the trigger. There was a stran-gled squawk then a puff of black feathers drifted by.

"Clem… Did you just shoot a bird?" Harper asked.

"That I did."

"Excellent shot too," the captain said. "You must be a hunter."

I laughed. "That's an understatement."

"And why are we shooting crows?" the captain asked.

"Not crows. Ravens. And that one was tracking you."

"Tracking me?"

I looked at Harper who nodded, understanding washing over her face. "Trained birds, Captain," Harper explained. "Agent Louvel was right. The stationmaster must have sent it to follow you. Clever."

I nodded. "The bad ones always are."

Harper pulled out her map. "Captain, you should take this route," she said, pointing to her map.

"*Agent* Louvel?" the captain said, eyeing me more closely this time.

"Yes. And *Agent* Harper."

The captain nodded slowly. "Well, *Agents*, I think I got very lucky today. We're pleased to have you aboard *The Menapii*."

"Thank you," I replied.

"*The Menapii*. That's an unusual name. What does it mean?" Harper asked.

"It is the name of our ancient Belgic tribe. We were all Celts once, were we not? And there is nothing Celts love to do more than fight Vikings. But today, let's evade, shall we?" he said then called to his balloonman.

The balloon filled with hot air, lifting the ship higher.

The captain studied Harper's map once more, reset his instruments, and then banked the ship starboard.

Leaving them, I went to the prow of the ship where I could get some air while I waited for Mrs. Martin's brew to start working in my stomach. Holding on to a rope, I stared out at the sky, letting the wind caress my cheek.

I closed my eyes, remembering that soft voice that had called my name. The voice had been sweet and feminine, the air perfumed with apple blossoms. What had I heard? The otherworld? The land of the Seelie? The Golden Troupe was said to use the standing stones and mounds to pass from our world into theirs. And worse, so did the Unseelie, though they had not been seen in the realm since Victoria took the throne. But I didn't know much about them. The fey had nothing to do with my beat. And as far as I knew, the Seelie were almost never in the realm.

Then what or who had called to me?

And how had they known my name?

CHAPTER 15
The Calvary

The airship *Menapii* arrived in port at Edinburgh in the early evening. Rather than returning to the inn, Harper and I headed directly to Shadow Watch. This time, we went to the front entrance. Expecting to be taken downstairs, we were surprised when we were asked to wait. A messenger went below. Immediately thereafter, Agent Walsh appeared.

"Good to see you both," Agent Walsh said. "Please, step inside," he said, motioning for us to join him in the lift. "We were afraid something happened to you."

Harper and I climbed into the lift. Agent Walsh activated the levers, and to my surprise, we ascended.

"Sorry to cause any concern. The *Jacobite* was too slow, so we sent her home. I need to talk to Agent MacGregor. We were thinking—" I began.

"That will have to wait. I've been instructed to bring you along as soon as you arrived."

"Bring us along where?"

"Your flying wolves struck again, and this time, they torqued off the wrong target."

"What happened?"

The lift dinged, and we exited into a long hallway on the upper, closed floor of Edinburgh Castle.

There were guards everywhere.

"What's happening?" Harper asked.

"We have a guest," Agent Walsh said as we approached the door at the end of the hall.

The guard standing there opened it to reveal several Shadow Watch agents, Agent MacGregor, Agent Hunter, Captain Martin, and Queen Victoria.

The Queen was standing at the window, frowning at the sky. She turned when she heard the door open.

Casting a quick glance at Agent Hunter who seemed to breathe a sigh of relief when he spotted Harper and me, I dropped into a low curtsey, Agent Harper following suit.

"Yes, yes," the Queen said distractedly. "I was about to send someone to look for you, Agent Louvel. Very glad to see you're still alive. Well, it seems you haven't been able to stamp out that trouble in the aether just yet."

"No, Your Majesty. But Agent Harper and I have

discovered the location of their base on North Ronald-say. We've also discovered how they are tracking marks."

"That, at least, is welcome news."

"Has something happened?" I asked, looking from the Queen to Agent Hunter.

"The airship *Fenrir* commandeered the Crown's ship, stole several items that were intended as part of the dowry for Princess Vicky, and made off with the Crown's treasure," Agent Hunter explained.

Hell's bells. Harper and I might have saved the cargo of the *Menapii*, but apparently, the *Fenrir* found a better mark in the process.

The Queen turned to Captain Martin. "You said you had the *Fenrir* in your sights, Captain. What happened?"

"She's too fast," Captain Martin said. "The *Jacobite* is powerful but too big to keep up with the *Fenrir*. The *Fenrir* has a longship design and is as fast as any racing ship. Her guns are not her strength. It's her speed. They pulled up into the clouds and were gone before we even got a run on her."

Queen Victoria looked at me.

I nodded.

"And if we can find a way to catch them, can you end this?" she asked me.

"The wolves may be strong, but they're no worse

than what we've already dealt with. We just need to catch them first."

Queen Victoria nodded. "MacGregor, go now and get the Watch ready. Captain Martin will take you to North Ronaldsay. If you find the *Fenrir* in port there, burn it to the ground. Otherwise, arrest everyone you find at their hideout and recover my treasure."

"Yes, Your Majesty," Agent MacGregor said, motioning for Captain Martin, Agent Walsh, and the other Shadow Watch agents to follow him from the room.

"And if the *Fenrir* is not at port?" Agent Hunter asked the Queen.

Queen Victoria laced her hands behind her back and paced the room.

We all waited.

And waited.

Agent Harper shifted uncomfortably beside me.

I cast a glance at Agent Hunter. To my surprise, he was looking at me. He smiled softly.

"Fine," Victoria said, resting her fingertips on the edge the table. "Fine. If we need to be fast, we'll be fast. Very well then. Someone bring me Lily Stargazer."

CHAPTER 16
The Infamous Lily Stargazer

There was not a child in all the land who didn't know the name Lily Stargazer. The infamous airship racer, the first female pilot to win a World Grand Prix and a multi-year winner of the British Airship Qualifying, was a legend. From guttersnipe to the lover of Lord Byron and an award-winning pilot who once dove out of an airship to save a fellow racer, we all knew Lily Stargazer and her ship, also named *Stargazer*. Hell, when we were kids, we'd try to run "faster than the *Stargazer*." But what had happened to the legendary woman?

All I knew was that she'd once raced in an around-the-world event and afterward, disappeared. I assumed she was either dead or off drinking rum in Bermuda— she was somewhat renowned for her carousing. She'd be in her fifties by now. The fact that Queen Victoria sent someone to fetch her surprised me more than I could hide. How in the hell did Queen Victoria know where Lily Stargazer was?

The Queen sent a runner to the Bank of Scotland—why, I had no idea—then Agent Harper and I went with Agent Hunter back downstairs to brief Agent MacGregor. At least a dozen Shadow Watch agents had been assembled. Harper hastily drew a map of the island for Agent MacGregor while I went to chat with Agent Walsh who was suiting up for the mission.

"Any advice, Agent Louvel?" he asked as he checked his weapon.

"Silver bullets. Lots of them."

Agent Walsh smirked. "That's a given."

"If you will strike, strike before dusk. They are weaker in daylight, unable to shift until the moon comes out. And they are weakest at midday."

"Thank you, Agent Louvel," he said then looked behind me. "Sir," he said, inclining his head.

I turned to find Agent Hunter there.

"Good luck on the mission, Agent Walsh. Fair bit more teeth than your usual beat," Agent Hunter said.

"That's for certain. At least I won't have to lug salt around. Thank you, sir," he told Agent Hunter then looked once more at me. "Agent," he said then joined Agent MacGregor.

"What's his usual beat?" I asked Agent Hunter.

"Spirits."

"Ghosts?"

Agent Hunter nodded. "Nasty ones, too."

I eyed my new boss. Had he always had that smattering of freckles across his nose and cheeks? He was so poised, so polished. The freckles gave him an earthy quality that I had somehow missed before. And those eyes… I had never seen eyes bluer.

I suppressed the sigh that wanted to escape my lips. He really was very handsome. And from what I saw, also very hardworking. It seemed like he was always at the office. He wasn't married—Agent Greystock had deemed it necessary to inform me of that tidbit—but wasn't he at least attached? I mean, who wouldn't want a man like him? He was prim, sure, but a prim man could be fun to—

"How is Agent Harper working out?" Agent Hunter asked, interrupting my completely inappropriate thoughts.

I tried to wipe off the very unseemly smile that had crept up on my face.

"Ah, yes. Very well, sir."

"We've arranged for her to rotate between divisions until we find the right placement. She did ask for you first."

"She's handy in the field." And she was. But she wasn't Quinn. The fact that I hesitated at the *Fenrir's* base was telling. Sure, it made sense to let the captain think he had not yet been discovered, but it would have been easier to take half the crew out then and catch the rest aloft. The truth was, I hesitated because I didn't want to get Harper killed.

"But?"

Hell's bells. How had he read between the lines? "The job can get ugly. I'm not sure she's ready for that."

Agent Hunter nodded, his manner such that he shared my thoughts.

"Agent Hunter," a runner called, rushing across the room. "Her Majesty asked for you and Agents Harper and Louvel. Their ride is coming in now."

That was quick.

Agent Hunter nodded then turned to me. "Shall we go meet Lily Stargazer?" he asked, raising and lowering his eyebrows, unable to hide his excited expression.

I chuckled then turned and motioned to Harper. The three of us, all of us trying to hide our childish glee, went together to the lift. Every one of us tried to keep our decorum. But halfway up the lift, Harper popped with an excited laugh.

"Sorry, I just couldn't help it. Lily Stargazer. Can you believe it?" Harper said.

I turned and looked at Agent Hunter who smiled at me.

And only at me.

A warm, happy, and much unexpected excited feeling filled my stomach.

I patted Harper on the back. "Just try not to embarrass us."

WE WAITED ON THE ROOF OF THE TURRET WITH HER Majesty and a fleet of guards, watching as an airship floated in. I eyed the shape of the ship. It was a single prop racing ship, but it wasn't the famous *Stargazer* with its triskelion symbol on the balloon. This airship's insignia was a swan.

The Edinburgh Castle crew rushed in to take the lead ropes. A moment later, someone tossed over a rope ladder. The crew appeared at the side of the ship. I spotted two men and a young woman—too young to be Lily Stargazer.

The crew on the airship talked—more argued from the looks of it—and talked and talked.

Queen Victoria frowned at the ship.

A moment later, a fourth person appeared—a woman in her fifties wearing a cap. She and a young man with black hair descended from the airship.

I cast a sidelong glance at Harper who was biting her lip.

Agent Hunter cleared his throat, then cleared it again.

The pair climbed down then went to the Queen. The woman dropped into a polite but brief curtsey to the Queen, the man bowing. The Queen, who was standing a few feet from us, spoke in low tones to the pair then they turned and headed toward us.

I'd only ever seen sketches of her, but the infamous airship racer was renowned for her beauty. Lord Byron, her one-time lover, had once remarked that Lily Stargazer was more beautiful than the Goddess Aphrodite. That was one of only a few times he'd ever spoken publically of her. Of course, most people speculated that his poem "She Walks in Beauty" was about the pilot, but no one really knew for sure. Their love affair appeared to have been both very real but also very secret.

Harper tittered a little, seemingly unsure if she should step forward and introduce herself.

Her Majesty motioned for us to follow them, but did not stop to make introductions.

Dressed plainly in boots, trousers, a long-sleeved shirt, and her trademark cap—complete with its clockwork lily pin—Lily Stargazer passed us by. And never gave us a second glance.

The young man who accompanied her, however, gave us a brief but polite nod.

Agent Hunter motioned for Harper and me to follow along. To my surprise, he set his hand on the small of my back to gently guide me forward.

"Can you believe it?" Harper whispered in my ear.

My thoughts scrambled by the unexpected touch, I raised an eyebrow at her. "Believe what?"

Harper swallowed a nervous laugh, making an odd chortle sound in the process, then whispered, "Lily Stargazer just snubbed us. I love her."

The young man who accompanied the airship racer, walking just ahead of us, chuckled but didn't look back.

I cast a gaze up at Agent Hunter who smiled at me.

Lily who?

CHAPTER 17

Up Yours

Whatever Queen Victoria thought was going to happen obviously wasn't going to come about as easily as she expected.

Agent Harper, Agent Hunter, and I waited on a bench outside a closed chamber door. On the other side, a heated argument was underway. The young man who had accompanied the airship racer waited with us. He stood by the door, seemingly unfazed by the shouting coming from inside.

I could only catch a scant few words: *duty, obligation, Arcadia, warden, now,* and *ridiculous.*

That was enough to get something of the picture.

It was only after I heard one more word, *Byron,* that the fighting ended.

This word, I noticed, also caught the attention of the young man waiting outside. He frowned heavily.

It seemed like forever before the door finally opened.

A red-faced Lily Stargazer appeared. She motioned to the young man, giving him a tender and apologetic look, then turned to us.

"Who's coming?" she asked abruptly.

Harper and I rose.

"We are," I told her.

"Let's go."

Agent Hunter looked back toward the Queen.

I followed his gaze. Queen Victoria inclined her head to me then motioned for me to go on.

"Be careful, Agent Louvel," Agent Hunter told me. "And Agent Harper."

"Thank you, sir," Agent Harper said then turned and followed Lily Stargazer.

I smiled at him then turned to leave.

Without another word, we followed Lily Stargazer back outside.

Shaking myself from the morass of emotions toying with my heart and mind, I quickened my step and joined the young man. He was just a bit older than me, dark-haired with light eyes, and had a complexion that looked more Italian than British.

"Clemeny," I told him, sticking out my hand.

"Orlando," he said, shaking my hand. "Don't mind my mum. She's out of sorts."

Mum?

"You'd be out of sorts too if you knew where she was sending us," Lily replied.

"I don't suppose you'll be telling me anytime soon," Orlando answered.

Lily laughed. "Oh, no. I tell you all at once. Can't wait to see what Angus has to say."

"That bad?" Orlando replied.

Lily laughed.

Orlando gazed at me, a smile behind his eyes. "And just what mischief are you mixed up in, Clemeny?"

Lily cast a glance over her shoulder. "She's a Rude Mechanical. So, the worst kind."

Orlando chuckled.

I looked back at Harper. Lily was mistaken. I wasn't a Rude Mechanical. I just worked for them.

Harper also noticed the confusion. She opened her mouth to say something but then thought better of it.

Walking behind the airship racer, I thought about her words.

What if she wasn't mistaken?

My brow furrowed as I thought it over.

What, exactly, did Lily Stargazer know?

CHAPTER 18
What Clemeny Saw

"So, we're hunting another airship," Angus asked. Angus, who was not as well-known as the pilot, had still received notoriety as being part of the winning crew of the airship *Stargazer*. He was about the same age as Lily, maybe a bit older. He had a heavy Scottish accent, a bald head, and was wearing a kilt and a frown.

"Yes," Lily answered.

"And when we find it, what will we be doing?" Angus asked.

Lily looked at me.

"We'll be downing it, if possible. Her Majesty wasn't specific on whether or not she wanted the crew alive or dead. Dead will be easier."

"Her Majesty does know this isn't a warship, right?" Orlando asked.

"Light weapons, I was told," Lily said then looked at me. From the expression on her face, I could see she already knew that this was something of a lie.

"That's true, on our side. I would expect them to be well rigged. We need to run up on them and get the drop. In the end, they are airship pirates. And right now, they are the realm's most wanted pirates."

"Vikings," Harper corrected under her breath.

I gave Harper a sidelong glance and coughed lightly. The last thing I wanted Lily Stargazer to know was that she was about to run up on some Vikings.

"Oh, aye, airship pirates, that's all. Of course. Lily, you know who they are, right? With them, nothing is what it seems. You should know that by now," Angus said, frowning at Lily.

"I do, which is why we will get them where they need to go then leave. We're not involved. Understand?" Lily asked me, her voice stern.

"Understood."

Lily looked up at the burner basket where a young woman with long, curly black hair and big blue eyes looked down at us. "We are not involved, you understand?" she told the girl.

The girl, who had been eyeing us with wide-eyed fascination, frowned at the infamous airship racer. "Yes, Mum. Of course," the girl said then turned away, rolling her eyes.

Mum? There were two?

Lily frowned then gave Orlando a knowing look.

He also eyed the girl suspiciously.

"All right. Let's get it over with," Lily told Angus then headed to the wheelstand.

"What is the name of this ship?" Harper asked Orlando who'd gone to the side of the airship to pull up the lead ropes.

"The *Aphrodite.*"

I eyed the balloon. A large swan had been painted thereon. I pulled out Mrs. Martin's flask and took a drink as the airship started to lift off.

"Nervous, Agent?" Lily asked.

I looked back at her. For once, she was smiling.

I shook my head. "Not spirits. Ginger."

"Ginger?" Lily chuckled. "Don't vomit on my ship, if you please."

"I'm trying not to. Thus, the ginger."

Lily grinned. "Well, where are we going?"

Harper pulled out her map and headed over to the racer. "Here," she said. "I'd expect them in this area. If they spy the *Jacobite*, they'll stay aloft. But they should be somewhere here. If we see the ravens, we'll know we're close."

"Ravens?" Lily asked.

Harper nodded. "They have an unkindness of

ravens, trained birds. The birds hunt out other ships and report back to the *Fenrir*."

"You hear that, Angus? These pirates use ravens to hunt their prey," Lily yelled to the open hatch of the gear galley.

"Oh, aye. I heard that. I told you so," the gear galley man yelled in reply.

Lily huffed a laugh. "Better take a seat, Agent Louvel," she said as she turned her ship north. To my surprise, Lily then pulled on a pair of goggles that looked a bit like the night optic array I wore. There was an odd green glimmer as she adjusted them. She scanned the horizon, apparently looking for something that remained unseen to me.

Harper took a seat not far from the wheelstand.

I held on to a rope and followed Lily's gaze as she guided the airship toward… What? A ray of sunlight. I frowned. Was she looking for wind?

The airship turned, and a moment later, a strange gust picked up from behind and propelled the ship forward. Quickly.

My legs buckled, and I took a couple of clumsy steps as I fought to regain my balance.

Lily chuckled. "I told you to take a seat."

I looked from her to the clouds around us. They seemed far too still for the velocity pushing us. "Where is that wind coming from?" I asked.

"Just a south wind," Lily said casually, but a smirk played on her lips.

The girl in the burner basket chuckled, earning her a reproachful glare from the pilot who was, apparently, her mother.

Orlando grinned at me then went belowdecks with Angus.

The bottoms of my feet were tingling, and the roots of my hair felt charged with energy.

I slipped off my eyepatch then pulled out my night optic array. There was something here I couldn't see. I moved to pull the optic on, but then I stopped.

While my good eye saw nothing more than the sun, clouds, and sky, my mooneye saw something more. I wouldn't have even noticed it if I hadn't been looking for it, but directly before the ship was a glimmer of light, like a parallel ray of sunshine. It seemed to be coming from the ground, emanating from the land itself. Frowning, I looked behind us. It was there as well. And the *Aphrodite* was flying along its course.

I turned and looked at Lily.

She met my gaze. From behind the goggles she wore, I could see her eyes take in my mangled face. To my relief, I didn't spy an expression of pity. More, there was an acceptance in her gaze that told me she understood that life was not always easy, kind, nor fair. And that, sometimes, gifts are born from pain.

"You see?" she asked.

I nodded. I wasn't sure what I was seeing, but there was something there. A line of energy. And the airship racer had tapped into it and was riding on it.

"Have a seat. We'll be there soon."

My optic still in my hand, I went and sat beside Agent Harper.

"What is it?" Harper asked.

I looked from the airship racer back to my partner. In truth, I didn't exactly know what I was seeing. It was something that, as much of what my mooneye saw, was both in this world and not of this world. Whatever this strange energy was, it propelled us forward. Quickly.

"Nothing," I said then pulled my night optic array on. "Nothing."

CHAPTER 19

The Aphrodite

arper kept one eye on her pocket watch and another on the landscape below. "We're making incredible time," she said, looking confused. "I guess what they always said was true. No one is faster than Lily Stargazer." She cast a suspicious glance at the pilot.

If there was one thing for sure, working for the Red Cape Society taught you to mistrust everything. Nothing was ever what it seemed.

When I looked at Lily, however, I was very confident that she was human. In fact, being in the presence of such a legend was very sobering. She was human, and from the feeling I got from her, painfully human.

I wanted to ask more times than I could count why she wasn't flying the famous *Stargazer*. Maybe she'd retired the ship. Maybe she realized it was too recognizable. Or maybe the *Aphrodite* was more equipped for this kind of fast flying. Something told me, however, that Lily Stargazer didn't like questions, so I didn't ask.

"We're coming up on Thurso," Lily told us.

Harper rechecked her pocket watch. "Already?"

Lily nodded.

"We may have outpaced the *Jacobite*," Harper told me then went to the pilot. "Steer clear of the shipping lanes. Go this route. We need a look at North Ronaldsay, but we need to stay out of sight."

"Clouds will be thick north of the island," the girl in the basket said.

Lily frowned at her once more.

I suppressed a chuckle, seeing my Grand-mere's scolding expression on the pilot's face. Did all mothers and daughters have that underlying tension?

Lily guided the ship away from the glimmer of light we were currently following to a course that would send us around the north tip of the island.

"Up thirty percent," she told her daughter who readily complied.

"Angus, drop speed," she called to the gear galley.

There was a click as the propeller at the back of the ship slowed almost to a stop. When the balloon began to fill, the ship coasted to a halt then started to lift into the clouds. The quick drop in acceleration followed by the lift caught my stomach off guard, and for a split second, I thought I might throw up.

Hell's bells. No, no, no.

I inhaled deeply, exhaling slowly, willing myself not to chunder on the deck of Lily Stargazer's ship.

Pulling out the flask, I took another sip.

The air cooled as we lifted into the clouds. Suddenly, it grew misty. The sun, entirely occluded by the clouds, gave everything an odd grey sheen trimmed in gold.

Checking her instruments, Lily made a slight adjustment to the course.

Orlando appeared from belowdecks once more. This time, he carried two guns which he started loading. The first was a long rifle...or so I thought. It had a unique design. It was like a hunting rifle but equipped with a revolver. His other weapon was a standard Colt 45 just like I carried.

Willing my stomach to be still, I crossed the deck of the ship and knelt to look at the long rifle.

"That's different," I said, eyeing it over. It looked like something Master Hart might dream up.

"Specialty item," he said with a knowing smile.

"But this I recognize," I said, motioning to his weapon. Pushing my cape aside, I gestured to my own weapon.

He nodded. "But those don't appear to be standard

issue," he said, tapping the silver vambraces on my forearms.

"Just a precaution."

"In case?"

"In case anyone gets too toothy," I replied.

Orlando raised an eyebrow at me.

I reached into my satchel and pulled out a box of bullets. "You'll want these."

He opened the box, looked inside, then looked back up at me. "Silver?"

I nodded.

He cast a quick glance at his mother who shook her head as she frowned.

Orlando loaded his gun with the silver bullets. "Interesting line of work you have."

"I believe we're recruiting."

He chuckled softly. "I'll keep that in mind."

The airship drifted slowly through the clouds. So far, no sign of the *Fenrir*, the ravens, or the *Jacobite*.

Lily kept the *Aphrodite* moving at a slow pace as she crept through the clouds. It was so silent. In a way, it was peaceful. The air was crisp, a soft mist caressing my face. And the wind was clean. I inhaled deeply, blessing Mrs. Martin once again.

I cast a glance back at Lily Stargazer.

She was gazing out at the clouds, the strange green goggles on her face. Her brow was furrowed. A moment later, she went to a storage cabinet not far from the wheelstand and pulled out a small case. I couldn't see what she was doing, but she returned shortly with something in her hands.

Lily went to the side of the ship. To my surprise, she whispered toward her closed hands then released…a bird? I didn't know what she'd released. I saw a flash of glimmering gold as something small and fast flew from her hands.

Harper, who had also been watching, strained to see.

Lily folded her arms across her chest and stood frowning at the clouds.

"Mum?" the girl in the basket called.

"Let's give her a minute," Lily replied.

I looked at Harper who shrugged.

A few moments later, I heard an odd buzzing sound then saw a flash of light as something bright moved toward the ship. It flew fast, first around the girl in the basket—who chuckled happily—then toward me.

The fast flying creature stopped a moment, hovering before me.

It was…a fairy. A clockwork fairy.

The finger-sized clockwork creation fluttered on thinly crafted metal wings. The tiny fey thing bowed to me then went back to the airship racer.

Too far away to see what was transpiring between the racer and the clockwork fairy, I could just make out a strange ringing sound. The airship racer nodded then went back to the wheel. The tiny fair woman disappeared back into the clouds once more.

"Well, seems we're just on time," Lily said.

"On time for what?" Harper asked.

"The battle. Better take another sip, Agent Louvel," she said then motioned to the girl in the balloon basket.

The girl grinned at me. "Sorry," she said and then turned a lever on the burner, shutting it off.

There was this brief moment when nothing happened.

And then, we began to fall.

Fast.

CHAPTER 20

Down She Goes

I closed my eyes as the ship—and my stomach—went hurtling down.

"Get ready," Lily called. "Angus?"

"On it, Lily."

She must have motioned then—I couldn't see because my eyes were still closed as I prayed to any god who would listen—because a moment later, I heard a loud hiss as the balloon began to inflate. Just like when a kite catches the wind, there was a tug. Suddenly, the terrible downward descent stopped.

But the moment it did, I heard the sound of gunfire. A lot of it.

"Clemeny," Harper said, her voice full of alarm.

I opened my eyes to see we were just above the cove where Skollson's crew had been hiding out. There, the *Jacobite* was engaged in battle with the *Fenrir*. The

Viking ship was still docked and was currently on fire. Shadow Watch agents were on the beach, storming the cave. But so were Skollson's crew. Even though the moon wasn't out, the wolves were still stronger than three men. MacGregor had brought numbers. Good. He was going to need them.

There was a loud explosion followed by a cracking sound.

Harper gasped.

The *Fenrir* had launched a bomb at the *Jacobite*. A massive hole had ripped into the side of the ship. The ropes tying the *Jacobite's* balloon to the gondola had come partially undone. The airship tipped and began to fall toward the water.

At the same time, the *Fenrir* pulled out of port and turned to head across the land.

Racing to the prow of the *Aphrodite*, I scanned the *Fenrir*. The gondola was still on fire, but a light crew of five or so had taken off, Zayde Skollson at the wheel.

"Follow them," I called back to Lily.

Toward the trouble. Always toward the trouble.

Without another word, the pilot turned her airship to make chase after the *Fenrir*.

"Speed, Angus. Now," Lily called.

"Orlando, what's the range on that rifle?" I called.

Lifting the weapon, he rushed toward the front of the ship, joining me.

"Far, but my aim's not good enough to hit a man."

"One, those aren't men. Two, we don't need to shoot them. And three, if you do need to shoot them, use the other bullets," I said then looked at Harper who had joined us. "Could use Quartermain about now."

Harper smiled.

"If we shoot out their balloon, they'll crash, yes?" I called back to Lily.

"That will do it," she replied.

I looked at Orlando. "If you don't mind."

Steadying his weapon, he took aim through the scope. He inhaled then let out a long, slow breath. And then, he fired.

The gun rattled as it let out a barrage of bullets.

I stared at the *Fenrir.*

Skollson ran to the stern of the airship and looked back, his eyes flashing red.

The *Fenrir* shuddered as the balloon began to deflate.

"There's a hole. Yes. The tear is ripping open fast," Harper said as she gazed out her spyglass.

The propeller at the back of the *Fenrir* kicked into high speed as the ship tried to make some distance between us. At the same time, the Viking ship was losing altitude. Skollson turned and yelled to his crew.

"Can you get us over there," I called to Lily.

She nodded.

"They're going to crash," I told Harper. "We need to

ALPHAS AND AIRSHIPS

get on the ground. There are five of them on the ship. Kill or capture, either will work. Don't get bit."

I saw a flash of nervousness cross her face, but then she clenched her jaw, nodded, and grabbed her gun.

Lily moved the *Aphrodite* toward the *Fenrir*. The Viking airship was going down in the field where Harper and I had hidden. In the distance, I spotted the circle of stones. And, for the first time, I noticed that bright line of energy that seemed to emanate from them in the cardinal directions.

"There," I told Lily, pointing to the stones.

Understanding, she guided the *Aphrodite* toward the glowing light.

Once again, the ship powered forward quickly, making up the space between the *Fenrir* and us in no time.

The first of the wolves began to bail out as the *Fenrir's* rudder bumped the ground. Four more followed.

"You go after Skollson," Harper told me.

Grabbing a rope, she climbed up onto the side of the airship. With a nod, Harper jumped from the side of the ship and slipped down the rope. She rolled when she hit the ground then sprung up a moment later and looked all around. Spotting one of the Vikings trying to make his escape, she set off in a sprint after him.

"Mum," the girl in the balloon basket called.

A moment later, there was a loud boom and a flash of orange as the airship *Fenrir* crashed.

Turning the ship, Lily guided the *Aphrodite* toward the *Fenrir*. I looked back at her. There was a strange expression on her face. Her features blank, Lily stared at the burning airship, her eyes looking haunted.

"This is where I get off," I told Orlando then grabbed a rope. "Circle around. Harper may need you. Silver bullets, remember?"

He nodded.

Climbing up on the rail, I looked back at Lily.

The pilot nodded to me.

Taking a deep breath, I held onto the rope then jumped.

CHAPTER 21
Zayde Skollson

I gnoring the sharp, searing pains in my ankles, I hit the ground running. I couldn't let Skollson get away. Snatching up his crew was less critical. If you didn't take out the alpha, the pack could always be reformed.

Of course, he also could have died when the airship crashed.

But I seriously doubted I'd get that lucky.

As I raced toward the burning wreckage, I saw some wood shift and Zayde Skollson emerged from the rubble.

No, not lucky.

Pulling my gun, I took aim and pulled the trigger.

Miss.

Skollson turned around and glared at me, red flames in his eyes.

MELANIE KARSAK

Dammit. My aim was completely off.

And, because apparently, Skollson was just as much of a fool as I was, he turned and rushed me.

I paused and pulled out my second pistol which I always kept stashed in my boot. I inhaled, squinted my good eye closed, and looked out through my mooneye. I saw his silhouette as he advanced on me. Damn, he was fast. And big. And getting closer.

Exhaling slowly, I pulled the trigger.

Skollson let out a strangled howl.

Opening both eyes, I saw the werewolf's knee buckle. But still, he advanced.

Hell's bells.

Taking aim once more, I tried for the other knee.

But before I could get off a shot, something hit me hard from behind.

I gasped. One of my guns bounced out of my hand as something pushed me to the ground. I wriggled from the grasp of a second wolf.

Ah, there was lucky number thirteen, right where I least expected him. He must have bailed out then came looking for Skollson.

Pulling my knife, I turned on the werewolf.

Skollson, seeing his underling had gotten me in hand, turned and rushed across the field away from me. Coward.

The werewolf snarled at me, cursed me in Norwegian, and then attacked.

Stupid wolf.

I ducked. The brutish figure, expecting to make an impact, had thrown all his weight into the punch. I stuck out my leg, tripping him as I slid to the side. He stumbled stupidly then fell.

Moving fast, I snatched the silver handcuffs from my belt and jumped on the brute's back, pressing him into the ground. Grabbing his arm, I yanked his hand behind his back and slapped on the handcuff.

The wolf let out a howl.

"Now, enough of that already," I said, tugging on his other arm and snapping the cuff around his hand.

The wolf pulled away. Struggling to his feet, he turned and glared at me, cursing me in his native tongue as he winced in pain.

Crossing my arms, I rolled my eyes at him. "Look, first of all, I don't understand a thing you're saying. And two," I said, then moving quickly, I punched him as hard as I could between the eyes.

The wolf swayed a moment, his curses dying in his throat, then dropped.

"Good boy. Stay right there."

I turned and scanned the field. In the distance, I spotted the *Aphrodite* hovering not far from the cliff. I couldn't see Harper.

I also couldn't see Skollson.

I cast my gaze around. There was nothing here, and he couldn't have gotten that far away already.

My eyes came to rest on the standing stones. Picking up my gun, I turned and ran in that direction, my knife ready.

As I approached the stones, I cast my gaze on the grass nearby. The long blades were bent in a path leading into the stones. The broken grass led in but not back out. He was here.

I stood just outside the stones. I felt their energy, their vibration. All the hair on my arms had risen. My palms itched. Scanning the stones, I didn't see Skollson anywhere.

"Sorry about the ship. Couldn't let you just run off like that," I called. "Shame though."

I began to move slowly around the tall monoliths. The stones, which were a few feet taller than me and twice as wide, could easily hide a man.

There was no reply.

Damn.

I'd hoped that would provoke him.

"And your crew. Sorry about that too. Looks like Shadow Watch has them rounded up save a few stragglers. We'll be sending you back to Oslo."

"I'm never going back," the wolf growled in reply.

Ah, touched a nerve. "No? Nothing for you there? Alpha issues, I suppose."

No answer.

I moved slowly around the stones. Where was he hiding?

"Ah, not an alpha issue? Probably a bitch then. I have to tell you, I haven't met a bitch I like yet. Troublesome lot. I can understand your troubles."

"You don't know anything," Skollson grumbled in reply.

A moment later, a bright, fast-flying object appeared in the air before me. The clockwork fairy fluttered a moment in the air in front of me then zipped into the stones. I saw her fly around each of the monoliths then move toward the tomb at the center. She zipped around it then returned to me, floating in the air before me once more.

I had never, ever, seen a fairy in my life. Hell, I didn't know if such things existed or not. Where Lily Stargazer had acquired the clockwork creature, I had no idea, but the tiny, metallic fairy in front of me was very clearly motioning toward the center tomb.

I inclined my head to her.

She bowed to me then sped off in a glimmer of light back toward the *Aphrodite*.

I turned and stepped into the standing stones. Once

again, my palms and the bottoms of my feet began to itch. The sensation of energy surrounded me.

Skollson was probably armed. He definitely was going to try to kill me and escape. But he was also injured.

"Come on, Zayde, let's talk. You don't want to go back. I really don't want to have to kill you. What am I going to do with you?"

A soft wind blew then. But oddly, it didn't blow across the field. Rather, the breeze came from within the stones themselves. This time, however, it carried a foul smell. A nasty stench of sulfur and decay wafted out of the tomb.

"To us. Give him to us," a hissing voice called.

Oh, damn. Not again.

I approached the tomb from the back.

I could just catch Skollson's light breathing inside.

I jumped up onto the capstone of the tomb. Crossing my arms, I inhaled deeply then blew out the air. I tapped my foot. Now what?

"Come on, Zayde. No ideas?" I asked.

Below me, hiding within the tomb, I heard Skollson swear.

"Hey, Zayde, let me ask you something. What's a fylgja?"

"What?" he huffed.

"A fylgja?"

"Follower. Supernatural follower."

Ah. "Like an unkindness of ravens."

He huffed again but didn't reply.

"So, how long have you been a werewolf?" I asked.

"Too long."

"What were you before that?"

"It doesn't matter anymore."

"Doesn't it? I mean, if you were a cobbler then turned into a werewolf, I think that would make a difference. What if you were a page, a farmer, a soldier, or a sailor? Hell, maybe you were an artisan or a poet. Doesn't who you *were* shape who you *are* now? I mean, you're still one of us, just not quite the same, right? Why don't you come out, and we can chat about your future?"

"If I come out, you'll die."

"We'll see. Come on out. Let's talk. You'll find I'm quite reasonable."

"Tell that to Fenton."

"Well, he tried to make it personal. I'm not reason-able when it gets personal. A simple hustler is another thing entirely."

I trained my gun on the exit of the tomb and waited.

But I didn't have to wait long.

A moment later, the rocks under me shifted as the wolf put his back into the capstone, pushing it side-

MELANIE KARSAK

ways. I jumped off just as the capstone tilted. The stone slid to the side but did not fall off.

I turned, taking aim at Skollson, just as his fist collided with my arm.

At least he'd anticipated the fight.

A moment later, he punched me hard in the ribs. It was all I could do not to throw up. From the searing pain, however, I knew he'd broken my bones. I stumbled backward. But, anticipating he'd throw another punch, I ducked around behind him. Turning, I kicked him in the back. He tumbled toward the rocks, barely stopping before he collided with a monolith.

He turned. Growling, he advanced on me. I blocked with my left arm. And I was glad too. He had tried to take a bite out of me. His teeth connected with my silver vambrace. He recoiled in pain, his skin burning. His knees buckled out from under him.

A cold breeze blew, the bad smell along with it. The nasty smells of sulfur and rot filled the air. And this time, I saw a glow within the tomb.

"To us. Give him to us," the voices called.

Wherever these voices were coming from, it was decidedly not the same place I had sensed the last time I was here.

I advanced on the wolf, kicking him over.

My silver cuffs on his crewmate, I was either going

to have to knock Zayde out or kill him. Twirling my gun in my hand, I decided to go with the former.

The werewolf, who was bleeding profusely from his knee and his temple, the skin around his mouth red, backed toward the tombstone.

The vile wind blew once more, and this time, I saw dark shadows moving under the tombstone. I saw their hunched, shadowed forms and round yellow eyes.

"Zayde, stop," I called, gasping when the shadowy forms of the small creatures reached out to grab him.

"I won't let you take me alive," Zayde spat at me.

"No. Wait. Stop," I said, motioning toward the stones behind him.

"To us. Give him to us, Clemeny Louvel," the little voices said. And then, with long, claw-like hands, they grabbed him.

"No," I yelled.

Turning my gun once more, I took aim, shooting at the unknown assailants.

Zayde, still not understanding, threw himself flat on the ground. But the moment he did, he stared back into the tomb. His eyes went wide when he saw the creatures there.

The little creatures shrieked. "A curse upon you, Clemeny Louvel," one of them called then retreated into the shadows.

I rushed across the grass and looked into the tomb-stone, my gun raised.

They were gone. Whatever portal they had opened, they had already retreated back into it once more.

Zayde looked up, staring from me to the stones. "Did you… Did you just save my life?" he asked.

"Yes, and you're welcome," I said then turned and cold-cocked him with my gun.

CHAPTER 22

Mighty Aphrodite

I dragged the unconscious Viking to one of the standing stones. Digging into my bag, I pulled out the length of rope I carried. It would have to do for now. I tied the wolf to the stone. Then, pulling out the small bit of salt I always carried, I poured a circle around the werewolf. Whatever had come through those stones might come back. This would protect him.

Once I had Zayde settled, I raced back across the grass toward the *Aphrodite*.

Apparently, I was just in time too.

While I'd had a bit of luck, things were not going so well for Harper.

Not well at all.

With my magnification scope, I saw that Harper was

busy fleeing as five werewolves pursued her to the edge of the cliff.

Hell's bells.

I'd left her alone for five minutes.

I ran after her.

To my relief, I heard Orlando's gun rattling from the deck of the airship. It appeared that they were trying to give Harper some cover so she could make an escape. To where, however, I wasn't sure. If they lowered the airship for her to get on, the werewolves would just follow. Hell, they were better jumpers than humans. So that was not going to work. I hoped Lily would realize that. Chances were good she'd figure it out.

With only a few bullets left, I raced after the werewolves. Harper must have winged a couple of them as they were running along slowly behind the rest of the pack.

I paused and took aim at one of the werewolves who was moving like he'd already received a shot in the leg. Aiming at the other leg, I pulled the trigger.

The wolf howled then went down.

The others looked back but decided Harper was the better mark. She must have pissed them off. Either that or it was the red hair. For some reason, preternaturals really hated people with red hair. Which ironic given that Cyril was the biggest red-haired nightmare I'd ever met.

I ran past the wolf I shot. He was lying in the grass holding his legs and cursing at me.

I waived to him. "I'll be back," I called then rushed toward the others.

Harper was running out of ground fast.

Orlando's gun rattled then fell silent.

There was a flurry of activity aboard the *Aphrodite*, but I couldn't see what was happening.

A moment later, the airship lifted.

Harper slowed to a stop as her only means of escape evaporated before her eyes.

Dammit, dammit, dammit.

I aimed at the werewolf closest to me and shot, but he was too far away.

He looked back at me, his eyes wild, red flames bouncing. But then he turned and headed after Harper.

The first wolf reached her.

My lungs burned in my chest, and my heart beat hard.

Dammit, she was going to get killed.

Harper threw a punch. The hit landed so well it surprised the wolf and me. The wolf stumbled back, clutching his nose.

"Harper," a female voice yelled from above. I looked to see the hatch on the bottom of the airship *Aphrodite* was open. Angus and the black-haired girl who operated the balloon were just inside.

A moment later, a figure dropped out of the bottom of the airship.

Attached to a lead of rope, the young girl who'd been working the balloon swung from the belly of the airship toward my partner.

Lily Stargazer raced to the rail of the ship. "Georgia," she screamed, a look of shock on her face.

A split second later, she disappeared back onto the airship.

Georgia swung low, reaching out and snatching Harper from the ground.

"Now, Angus," the girl yelled the moment she'd grabbed my partner.

I heard the winch on the gears of the airship grind, and a moment later, Harper and Georgia were pulled back up into the airship. The airship quickly ascended.

One of the wolves jumped and grabbed at them, pulling off Harper's red cape in the process, but nothing more.

My partner was safe.

Which was fabulous.

Except that left me alone with four angry werewolves.

CHAPTER 23
Run Clemeny Run

I slowed to a stop.

The werewolves turned and looked at me.

I smiled, gave them a little wave, then turned and ran.

All I needed to do was outpace them one at a time. I could take them out one at a time. Okay, sure, one of my guns was completely empty. The second? I had at least two shots left. Surely there were two shots in there.

I ran past the werewolf whose leg I shot once more. Grinning, I waved to him again.

Running ahead as best I could, I turned and shot.

Not expecting the move, I managed to hit the wolf closest to me in his upper thigh. He went down with a wince.

This, however, just seemed to make the others mad. They ran faster.

I took aim at the second brute.

Click.

Okay, there was only one shot left in there.

Not good.

If I got myself killed in front of Lily Stargazer, I was never going to forgive myself.

For once, I turned and ran away from the danger. As I raced along, I realized I was out of options. I was going to have to fight them hand to hand. I cast a gaze up at the sky. The *Aphrodite* was turning back, but not fast enough.

I slowed to a stop then turned.

Pulling out my blade. My thoughts went to my grand-mère. This was what she always feared. This.

I readied myself as the first werewolf approached. There were only three. I could handle three.

A moment later, however, I heard the rattle of a gun.

I looked up.

To my great surprise, another airship had descended from the clouds. It was held aloft by the red balloon of a Red Cape Society airship. And there, gun in hand, was Agent Hunter.

I almost swooned.

Almost.

Okay, maybe I swooned a little.

I turned and looked back at the werewolves who

stared up at the airship. They cast a glance from the airship to me and then they turned tail and ran.

Ugh. So much running.

Slipping down ropes, half a dozen Red Capes suddenly appeared. Passing me, they raced after the wolves.

Pausing to catch my breath, I looked up to see Agent Hunter slide down a rope. He crossed the grass and joined me.

"Thought you could use a little backup," he said with a smirk.

Nope, not swooning again.

"What? I had this handled."

"Was that the *Jacobite* I saw on fire?"

"Maybe. But *I* wasn't on the *Jacobite*. *I* was on the *Aphrodite*. And *we* shot down the *Fenrir*."

"Where's Harper?"

"On the airship," I said, pointing at the *Aphrodite*, which was coming up alongside the agency airship.

"And Skollson?"

"Left him tied to a rock over there," I said, pointing to the standing stones as I tried to catch my breath.

Agent Hunter chuckled. "I see," he said then laced his hands behind his back. "Seems like you didn't need me after all."

I grinned. "And why did you come, sir?"

"Just… On a hunch."

"A hunch?"

Agent Hunter shrugged, but a smile played on his lips all the same.

"I like your hunches, Agent Hunter."

"I like your work, Agent Louvel."

"Shall we go clean up this mess?"

"Before the moon comes out? Sounds like a grand idea."

CHAPTER 24

Gazing at Stars

The rope ladder leading up to the *Aphrodite* wagged in the breeze. My fellow Red Capes rounded up the crew of the *Fenrir*, including Zayde Skollson, who looked in my direction when they loaded him aboard the agency airship. The expression on his face was an odd tangle of anger, annoyance, and gratitude.

"Where are they headed?" I asked Agent Hunter.

"Her Majesty wants them sent back to Oslo."

I sighed. "From what Lionheart told me, it's likely they'll just get a slap on the wrist. We could be plucking him out of the sky again very soon."

Agent Hunter gave Skollson a long look. "No. Something tells me he won't be tempted to tangle with *Little Red* again."

"I'm the one with broken ribs. *I'm* not too keen on tangling with *him* again any time soon."

Agent Hunter eyed me carefully, his expression full of concern. "Are you serious?"

I nodded, gently touching the ribs on my left side. "Yeah, definitely broken."

"We'll get you to the surgeon in Edinburgh."

I shook my head. "If it's all the same to you, I'm really, really ready to head back to London. I have someone there who can patch me up."

Agent Hunter smiled sympathetically at me. "As you wish."

Harper and the crew of the *Aphrodite*—save Angus who was still on the ship—made their way toward Agent Hunter and me.

"And how was she?" Agent Hunter asked under his breath.

I raised an eyebrow at him. Apparently, Harper and I weren't the only ones who were star-struck. "Interesting."

He nodded. "That's what I figured. And fast. You must have arrived right behind the *Jacobite*."

"That we did."

"Interesting indeed."

"You have no idea." I smiled at the young woman who Lily Stargazer had called—well, more shouted—

Georgia. "We owe you a huge debt of gratitude," I told the girl. "You saved my partner's life. Thank you."

Harper smiled generously at the girl.

The girl shrugged. "Seemed like the right thing to do."

Lily gave her daughter an exasperated and mildly amused look. She shook her head.

"Thank you for your help," I said, turning to the airship racer. "You and your crew," I said, turning to Orlando.

He inclined his head to me.

"Don't forget what I told you," I told Orlando.

He huffed a laugh. "I'll keep it in mind."

Lily turned to me. "Do you need a lift back to Edinburgh?"

"We have another ship coming in," Agent Hunter told her.

She nodded. "All right. Then I assume Her Majesty will be satisfied?"

Agent Hunter nodded.

"Right. We'll be off then. Agent Louvel," Lily said with a grin, turning to me. "No offense, but I hope we don't cross paths again any time soon."

I chuckled. "Understood. It… It was an honor to meet you."

She smirked. "Don't get sentimental, Agent. It

Huht

doesn't suit you," she said then turned to Harper. "Agent Harper."

Harper tried to say something, but it came out as a mangled mess that sounded something like, "Bigy-outhankfansorryI... Oh, bloody hell."

Lily laughed. "Nice to meet you too."

With that, Lily Stargazer motioned to her children, and the three of them headed back to the *Aphrodite*.

"Well, I almost died, but the former crew of the *Stargazer* saved my life. So, that makes it about equal," Harper said as she watched them head back to their ship.

"It was quite the experience, to say the least," I agreed.

I waved to Angus who gave us a friendly salute then headed back belowdecks.

"Well, at least you didn't throw up on Lily Stargazer's ship. That would have been...awful," Harper said with a laugh.

I frowned at her.

"Throw up? Agent Louvel, are you sick?" Agent Hunter asked.

"No," I said, hoping that Harper would shut up.

Harper grinned at me then turned to Agent Hunter. "Agent Louvel gets motion sick."

Agent Hunter turned to me. "Is that true?"

"Yes, but I'm fine now."

"You did all this while sick?" Agent Hunter asked.

"She was positively green," Harper said with a laugh.

"Oh my god, shut it."

Harper chuckled.

Agent Hunter gave me a sympathetic smile, an expression which made my stomach flop, and not in a bad way.

"There is the second ship," Harper said, motioning to another red-ballooned agency ship.

"Shall we pick up Shadow Watch and head home?" Agent Hunter asked.

I grinned. "Yes. But let's make sure Agent Walsh goes on that ship," I said, pointing to the airship full of werewolves headed on the long, uncomfortable ride to Oslo.

Agent Hunter raised an eyebrow at me.

"Can you help with that? Harper and I owe him a little thanks for his *hospitality*."

"As you wish, Agent Louvel," Agent Hunter said with a smirk.

"Ugh," Harper said, looking back at the remains of the *Fenrir*. "That's a mess."

"Indeed. You'll need to fill out Form 776 on that one, Agent Harper," Agent Hunter told her.

"Form 776? That's fifty pages long!"

"So it is."

I chuckled then looked back once more at the *Aphrodite* which was ascending into the clouds, taking the living legend—and her clockwork fairy—along with it.

CHAPTER 25

One too Many

After leaving the Shadow Watch agents at Castle Rock, Harper, Hunter, and I headed to the Edinburgh airship towers to take a second ship back to London. I was still nauseous, my ribs hurt, my busted lip still was sore, and I'd gotten a few new cuts along the way, but I was alive.

What more could I ask for?

As we made our way back down the Royal Mile to the towers, I spotted Ronald at the door of the White Horse Pub. He looked like he was just headed in to work for the night.

"Agent Louvel," he called.

I stopped a moment, Harper and Hunter waiting for me a discreet distance away.

"Should I get some extra potatoes on?" he asked with a smirk, motioning to the door of the pub.

While Harper looked away, trying not to pay attention to the scene, I could feel Agent Hunter's eyes on the brawny tapster and me. Suddenly, I felt like I wanted to sink into the ground.

"Thanks," I said. "Not today."

"Headed back to London already?"

I nodded. "Yeah. I've had enough action for now."

Ronald chuckled. "So I see. Want a drink first? On the house. You and your friends, of course."

I looked back at Agent Hunter. He was standing very still, his hands laced behind his back. Harper was just behind him. To my surprise, she flicked her eyes toward our boss and gave me just the slightest knowing look.

"Thanks, but no. We need to head back."

Taking the cue, Ronald nodded. "Well, maybe next time you're this way."

"Thank you," I replied, and with that, I rejoined the others.

We continued toward the towers. As we walked, my stomach filled with nervous butterflies. I hated the idea that Agent Hunter might think me a barfly, or a flirt, or whatever he thought. Ronald seemed like a nice enough guy, but still. Agent Hunter's good opinion of me meant a lot more than some random flirtation.

"You used to work this city. Ever been in there

before?" I asked Agent Hunter, motioning back to the pub.

"Can't say I have."

"Interesting place. I met the Loch Ness Monster there."

Agent Hunter stopped. "Sorry?"

"Eideard, the waterhorse."

"Was there? At the pub?"

I chuckled. "Yeah, he bought me a drink, pulled me out of a scuffle later on too. Nice chap."

At that, Agent Hunter smirked. "You, Agent Louvel, have a nose for trouble."

"I guess that's what makes me good at the job."

"I guess so," Agent Hunter replied, smiling lightly.

I cast a glance at Harper who grinned at me but didn't say another word.

CHAPTER 26
Making Plans

T
he next day, I found myself at the squash court at King's College. Since Lionheart hadn't yet warmed up to Harper, I decided to go on my own to let the alpha know that the skies above the realm were clear once more.

I slipped into the viewer's box just as Lionheart and Bryony had finished their match. This time, the werewolf had won. They chatted with one another as they went to put their rackets away. I was just about to open the small door leading onto the court when I stopped cold.

Lionheart stepped close to Bryony, setting his hand on her chin. He gazed down at her, and a moment later, leaned in and kissed her.

Taking my hand off the door handle, I stepped back into the shadows of the viewing box and stayed there.

When they finally let one another go, he whispered something in her ear.

Bryony smiled at him, squeezed his hand, then headed out of the court.

Lionheart finished cleaning up the equipment then turned and looked back at the viewer's box.

"Coming out, Agent Louvel?" he called.

There was a strange, sick feeling in my stomach. Jealousy? That was stupid. But it was there all the same. I didn't want Lionheart. I was a werewolf hunter, not a werewolf lover. But I liked that the alpha was fond of me. It made me feel…special.

"I was just trying not to interrupt," I replied as I joined him on the court.

"For that, I am obliged. After all, I have you to thank for the progression of things with Professor Paxton."

"Me?"

"I had, for some time, sensed her growing attachment. I had tried to ignore it, given my true condition, but it seems that my affliction is not an impediment to her affection."

"I'm glad to hear it," I replied, trying really hard to be as glad as my words suggested.

Lionheart smiled abashedly then turned and studied me more closely. "Well," he said then. "Looks like you found the flying wolf."

"So I did. He's flown back to Oslo, for now. The situation is in hand."

Lionheart inclined his head to me. "I expected no less, *Little Red*."

I smiled nervously. "Yeah. Thanks. Well, anyway, I just wanted to let you know. I won't keep you from your lady."

Lionheart inclined his head to me.

I turned and went to the door but paused just a moment. "Richard, what do you know about the druids?"

Lionheart shook his head. "Both before and after my time. A secret sect, really."

"Not unlike the Templars."

"No, indeed. Different flavor though."

I nodded.

"Go to the summer country, Agent Louvel. If you want to know about the druids, walk the lands of Arthur."

I nodded.

"And if you run across the Holy Grail, be a good sister-in-arms and snag it for me. I've only been looking for it for a few hundred years."

I laughed. "Of course. Good-bye, Sir Richard."

"Good-bye, Agent Louvel."

Reluctantly, I took the tram back across town to headquarters. There, I found Agent Harper at her desk, busily working on completing Form 776. Still nursing my sore ribs, I slowly sunk into my seat. My entire torso had turned the loveliest shades of yellow and purple.

"I left you Form 912 and Form 11," Harper said, pointing to the papers on my desk.

I picked up my fountain pen then set it back down. Leaning back in my chair, I scanned the room for Agent Hunter.

"He's gone already," Harper said without looking up.

"Sorry?"

"He got called out on a case first thing this morning. He stopped by though, asked where you were."

I looked at Harper.

She looked up at me then winked. "What? I'm observant."

I chuckled.

"I do have bad news though," Harper said.

"And that is?"

"I'm rotating to Cressida now," Harper said, referring to one of our colleagues who worked in magical artifacts. "She has a case. Hunter asked me to follow up with her when I'm done with the paperwork for the *Fenrir* case."

I smiled softly at her. I hated to let her go. "I'll miss you, but I am glad about one thing."

"What's that?"

"Hunter said you can join Cressida when you're done with the paperwork for the *Fenrir* case, right?"

"Yes, that's what he said."

Moving slowly, I rose. "Good."

"Why is that good?"

"Because he said when *you're* done with the paper-work. He didn't say anything about me."

"And just where are you going?"

"To my grand-mère's house. I have two broken ribs, a busted lip, and more bruises than I can count. I can't think of any place I'd rather be."

Harper laughed. "Fine, Clemeny. I'll finish it all."

"Thanks, Harper."

"Tell Cressida not to get too used to having you around. I'm going to need you back when you're ready."

Harper beamed a smile at me. "I already told Agent Hunter I'd rather just stay with you, but he wants me to finish my rotations."

"Makes me wonder what Agent Hunter's got planned for me."

"Oh, I definitely think he has plans for you. Not sure they're all work-related though."

"Oh my god, shut it."

Laughing, Harper said, "Go get some rest, Clemeny."

"Thanks, Harper. For everything."

She nodded then—thankfully—picked up the paperwork she'd left on my desk and set it in her own pile.

I turned and headed to the exit.

And just what did Agent Hunter have planned for me?

I couldn't wait to find out.

Continue Clemeny's Adventures in Peppermint and Pentacles

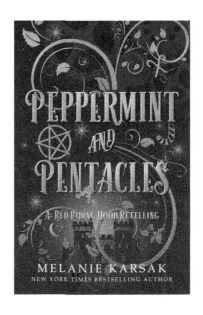

About the Author

New York Times and *USA Today* bestselling author Melanie Karsak is the author of *The Celtic Blood Series*, *The Road to Valhalla Series*, *The Celtic Rebels Series*, *Steampunk Fairy Tales* and many more works of fiction. The author currently lives in Florida with her husband and two children.

amazon.com/author/melaniekarsak
facebook.com/authormelaniekarsak
instagram.com/karsakmelanie
pinterest.com/melaniekarsak
bookbub.com/authors/melanie-karsak
youtube.com/@authormelaniekarsak

Also by Melanie Karsak

Shield-Maiden: Gambit of Blood

Shield-Maiden: Gambit of Shadows

Shield-Maiden: Gambit of Swords

Eagles and Crows

The Blackthorn Queen

The Crow Queen

THE HARVESTING SERIES:

The Harvesting

Midway

The Shadow Aspect

Witch Wood

The Torn World

STEAMPUNK FAIRY TALES:

Curiouser and Curiouser: Steampunk Alice in Wonderland

Ice and Embers: Steampunk Snow Queen

Beauty and Beastly: Steampunk Beauty and the Beast

Golden Braids and Dragon Blades: Steampunk Rapunzel

THE RED CAPE SOCIETY

Wolves and Daggers

Alphas and Airships

Peppermint and Pentacles

Bitches and Brawlers

Howls and Hallows

Lycans and Legends

THE AIRSHIP RACING CHRONICLES:

Chasing the Star Garden

Chasing the Green Fairy

Chasing Christmas Past

THE CHANCELLOR FAIRY TALES:

The Glass Mermaid

The Cupcake Witch

The Fairy Godfather

The Vintage Medium

The Book Witch

Find these books and more on Amazon!

Printed in Great Britain
by Amazon

42963562R00108